image comics presents
THE WALKING
DEAD™

CHARLIE ADLARD
PENCILER, INKER

CLIFF RATHBURN
GRAY TONES

TONY MOORE
COVER

For SKYBOUND ENTERTAINMENT

Robert Kirkman - CEO
J.J. Didde - President
Sean Mackiewicz - Editorial Director
Shawn Kirkham - Director of Business Development
Brian Huntington - Online Editorial Director
Helen Leigh - Office Manager
Feldman Public Relations LA - Public Relations

FOR INTERNATIONAL RIGHTS INQUIRIES, PLEASE CONTACT FOREIGN@SKYBOUND.COM

WWW.SKYBOUND.COM

IMAGE COMICS, INC.
Robert Kirkman - chief operating officer
Erik Larsen - chief financial officer
Todd McFarlane - president
Marc Silvestri - chief executive officer
Jim Valentino - vice-president

Eric Stephenson - publisher
Ron Richards - director of business development
Jennifer de Guzman - pr & marketing director
Branwyn Bigglestone - accounts manager
Emily Miller - accounting assistant
Jamie Parreno - marketing assistant
Jenna Savage - administrative assistant
Kevin Yuen - digital rights coordinator
Jonathan Chan - production manager
Drew Gill - art director
Tyler Shainline - print manager
Monica Garcia - production artist
Vincent Kukua - production artist
Jana Cook - production artist
www.imagecomics.com

THE WALKING DEAD, VOL. 2: MILES BEHIND US. Ninth Printing. Published by Image Comics, Inc. Office of publication: 2001 Center St., Sixth Floor, Berkeley, California 94704. For information regarding the CPSIA on this printed material call: 203-595-3636 and provide reference # RICH – 489263

PRINTED IN THE USA

ISBN: 978-1-58240-775-3

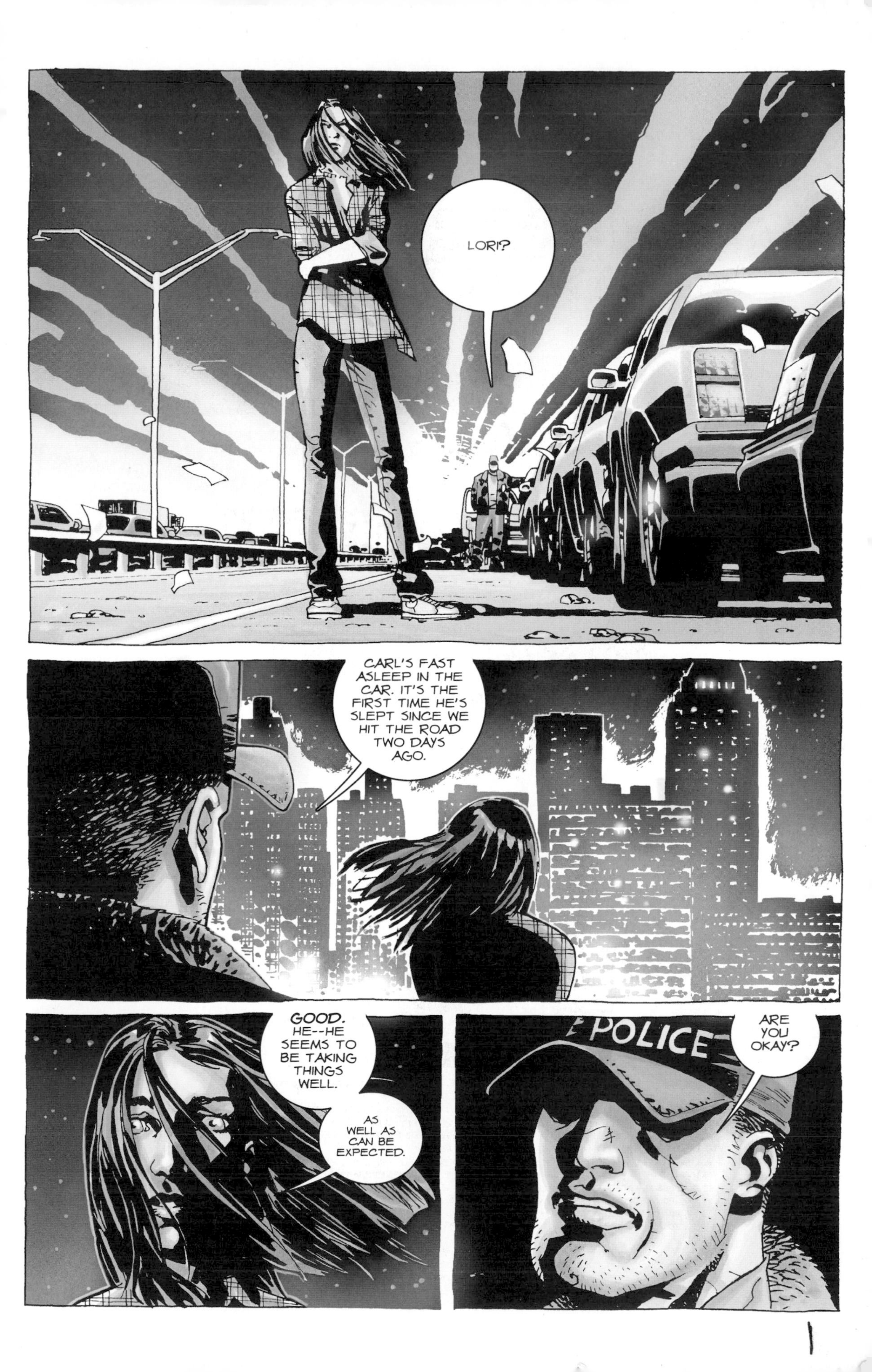
LORI?
CARL'S FAST ASLEEP IN THE CAR. IT'S THE FIRST TIME HE'S SLEPT SINCE WE HIT THE ROAD TWO DAYS AGO.
GOOD. HE--HE SEEMS TO BE TAKING THINGS WELL.
AS WELL AS CAN BE EXPECTED.
POLICE
ARE YOU OKAY?

LOOK AT IT... THE WHOLE CITY IS OVERRUN. WE CAN'T EVEN GET IN WITHOUT BEING ATTACKED. MY PARENTS ARE DEAD... EVERYONE THAT CAME TO THE CITY FOR PROTECTION IS DEAD. THEY'D HAVE TO BE.
NOBODY COULD SURVIVE THAT.
POLICE
AND RICK... THREE WEEKS HE'S BEEN IN THAT COMA. HE DOESN'T EVEN KNOW THIS HAS HAPPENED... AND WE LEFT HIM, TO COME HERE-- FOR THIS.
I'D SUGGEST JUST GOING BACK FOR HIM... BUT HE'S SAFE AT THE HOSPITAL. IT'S THE SAFEST PLACE FOR HIM, AND WE CAN'T HELP HIM IN HIS CONDITION.
BESIDES... IF THE GOVERNMENT IS GOING TO START CLEANING THIS PLACE UP SOON-- NEAR A MAJOR CITY IS THE BEST PLACE TO BE.
OH, SHANE. I CAN'T THANK YOU ENOUGH FOR COMING WITH US. CARL AND I WOULD NEVER HAVE MADE IT DOWN HERE ON OUR OWN. I'LL NEVER BE ABLE TO REPAY YOU.
I DON'T KNOW WHAT'S GOING THROUGH YOUR HEAD BUT I'M A WRECK. I DON'T REALLY KNOW HOW TO EXPLAIN IT.
WITH ALL THAT'S GOING ON... WITH RICK, AND MY PARENTS, AND THE WORLD... DON'T TAKE THIS THE WRONG WAY, BUT... I JUST FEEL SO...
...ALONE.

LORI... I'M SORRY... I DIDN'T MEAN--
I'M SORRY.
NO, SHANE... DON'T APOLOGIZE. EVERYTHING WE'VE BEEN THROUGH-- EVERYTHING WE'RE GOING THROUGH... I UNDERSTAND.
SHANE I-- I NEED YOU.
I NEED YOU.
OH, LORI...
I'VE WANTED THIS FOR SO LONG.
POLICE
PC

ALL RIGHT THEN.
...

PTOO!
YOU SON OF A BITCH.
WHAT A DAY, HUH?
LORI... SHE--SHE'S TAKING IT HARDER THAN THE REST OF US. I GUESS WITH THE TRIP DOWN HERE... HIM TAKING CARE OF HER AND CARL... SHE TRUSTED HIM.
HELL, WE ALL DID.
I NEVER WOULD HAVE THOUGHT HIM TO BE ONE TO SNAP LIKE THAT... HE JUST... LOST IT.
HE WAS MY FRIEND... PROBABLY MY BEST FRIEND. THIS SHIT WE'RE IN IS NOT TO BE TAKEN LIGHTLY. IF IT CAN CHANGE A MAN LIKE SHANE SO DRASTICALLY, WE'RE IN DEEPER SHIT THAN WE THOUGHT.
I JUST--
I BETTER HANG BACK... LET HER CATCH UP.
WE'LL TALK LATER.

HOW IS SHE DOING?
BETTER... BUT IT'S GOING TO BE A LONG TIME BEFORE THAT POOR GIRL IS GOING TO BE BACK TO NORMAL.
DALE, DO YOU THINK ANY OF US WILL EVER BE BACK TO NORMAL?
AFTER TODAY? NOT REALLY... AND SPEAKING OF WHICH... AND I'M NOT SAYING THIS TO SAY I TOLD YOU SO... I SAW THIS COMING. SHANE'S BEEN CHANGING SINCE YOU ARRIVED.
I THINK HE WAS IN LOVE WITH YOUR WIFE.
I KNOW. THE THINGS HE WAS RAMBLING ON ABOUT BEFORE HE TRIED TO SHOOT ME... THAT'S ALL THAT MAKES SENSE.
YEAH... BUT WHAT I'M GETTING AT IS THAT EVERYONE IN THE CAMP WAS STARTING TO GET WARY OF SHANE. THE ATTACKS, AMY--JIM... WE ARE READY TO MOVE THIS CAMP, RICK. WE LET SHANE CALL THE SHOTS BECAUSE HE WAS A COP... I'M AN OLD MAN, GLENN'S A KID, ALLEN... WELL... HE'S NOT LEADERSHIP MATERIAL.
WE NEED SOMEONE TO LOOK UP TO... TO MAKE US FEEL SAFE, ESPECIALLY THE WOMEN. I TALKED TO EVERYONE EARLIER... WE THINK THAT SOMEONE IS YOU.
OKAY THEN... GET SOME SLEEP. WE'RE MOVING CAMP TOMORROW.
WE'VE BEEN HERE LONG ENOUGH AS IT IS.
OH, AND ONE MORE THING... ANDREA'S BEEN KEEPING TRACK OF DAYS SINCE THIS WHOLE THING WENT DOWN. UNLESS SHE'S MESSED UP ALONG THE WAY--
TOMORROW IS CHRISTMAS.
DON'T TELL ANYONE! DO YOU HEAR ME? I DON'T WANT ANYONE TO KNOW. I DON'T WANT TO HAVE TO EXPLAIN TO MY SON THAT ON TOP OF ALL THIS OTHER SHIT... SANTA CAN'T FIND HIM.
LET'S JUST SKIP CHRISTMAS THIS YEAR, OKAY? I DON'T WANT TO UPSET THE KIDS.
OKAY... UNDERSTOOD.

DADDY?
YOU SLEPT PRETTY LATE, CARL. WE'RE ALL ALMOST DONE PACKING UP FOR THE BIG MOVE. YOU DOING OKAY?
IF YOU EVER WANT TO TALK ABOUT WHAT HAPPENED... YOU CAN TALK TO ME.
I KNOW, DAD.
SO IF YOU EVER WANT TO TALK... YOU'LL LET ME KNOW. OKAY?
UH HUH.

WE ALL READY TO GO?
I JUST NEED TO GET THE GAS FROM THE CARS INTO THE RV. WE'LL BE READY TO HIT THE ROAD AS SOON AS DALE'S READY.
I'M ALL SET. WE CAN GO RIGHT AFTER WE'RE GASSED UP.
OKAY. EVERYONE TAKE A GOOD LOOK AROUND THE CAMP AND MAKE SURE WE'RE NOT FORGETTING ANYTHING--
--AND THEN LET'S GET THE HELL OUT OF HERE.

IT'S A BUMPY RIDE, BUT WE'LL BE FINE AS LONG AS I TAKE IT SLOW. WE SHOULD BE ON THE ROAD IN NO TIME.
THANK GOD THE SNOW LET UP, EH?
HE'S GOTTA STOP SHITTING ON US SOMETIME, Y'KNOW?

WE ALMOST THERE?!
JUST A LITTLE FURTHER... UGH... AND IT'LL BE OUT OF THE WAY.

UNGH!
WE DON'T HAVE TO GET IT COMPLETELY OFF THE ROAD... JUST OUT OF THE WAY.
THEN I THINK WE'VE ABOUT DONE IT. YOU GUYS CAN GIVE IT A REST.
WHEW!
I DON'T THINK I COULD HAVE LASTED MUCH LONGER.
UH... RICK?
LOOK AROUND! SEE HOW MANY THERE ARE!
WE DON'T WANT TO GET SURROUNDED!!

WHOA! WHOA!
HOLD YOUR FIRE!!
OH, JEEZ, MAN!
OH, GOD-- WE COULD HAVE KILLED YOU!
I'M SORRY TO SNEAK UP ON YOU... ESPECIALLY IN THE DARK LIKE THAT. WE WERE WALKING ACROSS THE FIELD WHEN MY DAUGHTER, JULIE, SAW YOUR HEADLIGHTS.
WE DON'T SEE A LOT OF PEOPLE. LIVE ONES AT LEAST... NOT ANYMORE.
I HEAR YOU... I WAS STARTING TO THINK WE WERE IT.
I'M RICK.
TYREESE.
AND THIS HERE IS JULIE AND CHRIS... DO YOU GUYS HAVE ANY FOOD?

JULIE AND CHRIS ARE-- GOING STEADY? DATING? I DON'T KNOW THE CORRECT TERM ANYMORE. ANYWAY... CHRIS WAS STAYING WITH US WHEN EVERYTHING STARTED GOING TO HELL, FAMILY PROBLEMS. LONG STORY.
WE HAD A PRETTY GOOD SET UP BEFORE WE RAN OUT OF FOOD AND IT GOT COLD... WITHOUT HEAT, OUR HOUSE WAS AS COLD AS OUTSIDE. WE DIDN'T HAVE A FIREPLACE OR ANYTHING.
SO, A COUPLE WEEKS AGO WE SET OUT IN SEARCH OF FOOD.
WE THANK YA FOR WHAT YOU GOT HERE. WE HAVEN'T EATEN FOR A COUPLE DAYS.
DON'T MENTION IT, MAN. IT'S JUST GOOD TO SEE A NEW FACE. LISTEN. WE'RE CALLING IT A NIGHT HERE SOON AND I'M SURE WE COULD MAKE SOME ROOM IN THE RV FOR YOU IF YOU AND YOUR KIDS WANT TO STICK AROUND.
JUST FOR TONIGHT... OR LONGER, I THINK IT'S SAFER TO BE IN GROUPS, YOU'RE WELCOME TO TAG ALONG WITH US.
THAT'S KIND OF YA, RICK... BUT IF IT'S ALL THE SAME I THINK THE KIDS AND I WILL PROBABLY JUST SLEEP IN THIS CAR OVER HERE.
THEY'RE NOT TOO COMFORTABLE AROUND STRANGERS...
UNDERSTOOD. WE'LL SEE YOU TOMORROW THEN.
YOU'RE JUST INVITING A STRANGER TO SLEEP IN THE SAME ROOM AS US?
HE'S GOT KIDS WITH HIM, LORI.
SO DO WE. DON'T BE SO TRUSTING, RICK.

SORRY ABOUT THAT LAST NIGHT. ONE MINUTE I'M TELLING YOU WE HAVEN'T SEEN ANYONE... THE NEXT I'M USING "THE KIDS ARE AFRAID OF STRANGERS" AS AN EXCUSE TO NOT SLEEP IN THE RV WITH YOU.
IT'S JUST-- YOU CAN NEVER BE TOO CAREFUL, Y'KNOW. YOU GUYS COULD HAVE BEEN TRAVELING CANNIBALS FOR ALL I KNOW.
WHAT CHANGED YOUR MIND?
THE JURY'S STILL OUT.
I UNDERSTAND WHAT YOU'RE SAYING, THOUGH. THIS STUFF CHANGES PEOPLE. I JUST WATCHED MY BEST FRIEND FLIP OUT AND TRY TO KILL ME NOT A COUPLE DAYS AGO. I'D NEVER SEEN ANYONE ACT LIKE THAT... LET ALONE HIM. I WAS SO SHAKEN BY SEEING THE CHANGE IN HIM I ALMOST DIDN'T EVEN REALIZE THE DANGER I WAS IN.
I THINK WE'VE GOT SOME GOOD PEOPLE HERE... I THINK WE'RE GETTING BY OKAY... BUT HONESTLY... I JUST DON'T KNOW WHAT ANYONE'S THINKING.
TO ME, THAT'S SCARIER THAN ANY HALF-ROTTEN GHOUL TRYING TO EAT MY FLESH.
A COUPLE WEEKS AFTER THIS ALL STARTED... THE FIRST TIME WE RAN OUT OF FOOD, WE MADE A RUN DOWN TO A COUNTRY STORE ABOUT TWO MILES AWAY FROM OUR HOUSE. WE GOT THERE TO FIND THE PLACE TORN APART... IT'D BEEN LOOTED THREE TIMES OVER... BUT THERE WERE STRAY CANS ALL OVER THE PLACE. IT SEEMED SAFE ENOUGH SO JULIE, CHRIS AND I SPLIT UP... LOOKING THE PLACE OVER TO FIND AS MUCH FOOD AS WE COULD.
THERE WAS THIS NICE OLD MAN, GOTTA BE AT LEAST SIXTY. HE WAS ALWAYS SITTING IN FRONT OF THE STORE WITH BUDDIES CHATTING AWAY ABOUT GOD KNOWS WHAT... NICEST OLD MAN YOU'D EVER MEET. ALWAYS HAD A KIND WORD TO SAY. WHILE WE WERE SEPARATED, HE GOT A HOLD OF JULIE... PULLED HER INTO A BACK ROOM. SEEMS HE'D BEEN LIVING IN THE PLACE... WE HAD NO IDEA ANYONE WAS EVEN THERE.
THIS SWEET OLD MAN... THE FIRST THING HE THINKS OF WHEN HE FINALLY SEES OTHER PEOPLE... HE TRIED TO RAPE JULIE. HAD I BEEN TWO MINUTES LATER WHEN I FOUND THEM... HE'D HAVE DONE IT.
I KILLED THAT MAN, RICK. I WANTED TO... BUT I DIDN'T MEAN TO. I BEAT ON HIM... AND HE DIED.

JESUS, MAN... DON'T BEAT YOURSELF UP OVER THAT... YOU DID WHAT ANY FATHER WOULD HAVE DONE IN THAT POSITION.
I MAY BE A COP... BUT I DON'T LET RULES BLIND ME TO WHAT'S RIGHT AND WRONG. ESPECIALLY IN LIGHT OF OUR CURRENT SITUATION.
I'M NOT BEATING MYSELF UP BECAUSE I DID IT... I'M BEATING MYSELF UP BECAUSE I DON'T FEEL BAD ABOUT DOING IT.
YEAH-- THE END OF THE WORLD CHANGED HIM... BUT LOOK AT HOW IT CHANGED ME.
OH, SHIT.
ROAMERS.
ROAMERS?
OH... YEAH, UM. WHEN WE WERE CAMPED NEAR ATLANTA, WE WENT INTO THE CITY... MOST OF THE ZOMBIES JUST SAT AROUND, NOT DOING ANYTHING UNLESS PROVOKED. IT SEEMED MOST OF THEM WERE CONTENT TO SIT AND DO NOTHING UNLESS SOMETHING HAPPENS BY THEM.
THEN OUR CAMP WAS ATTACKED... A PACK OF THOSE THINGS JUST TORE THROUGH US, KILLED TWO OF OUR FRIENDS. SO I GOTTA THINK THAT THERE ARE OTHER KINDS OF ZOMBIES THAT ROAM AROUND, ALWAYS ON THE MOVE.
I FIGURE ROAMERS IS AS GOOD A NAME AS ANY.
THEY'RE COMING THIS WAY... WE GOTTA DO SOMETHING.
WE'VE GOT AN AXE IN THE RV IF YOU WANT TO GRAB IT. GUNS MIGHT ATTRACT MORE OF THEM.
THIS HAMMER HAS WORKED JUST FINE FOR ME SO FAR.

WE NEED TO SPLIT THEM UP... YOU GO THAT WAY AND TRY TO GET THAT ONE'S ATTENTION.
GOTCHA.

HEY, UGLY! OVER HERE!
GUH?

SHIT! LOOKS LIKE THEY'RE BOTH COMING FOR ME!

I'M ON IT.

THIS WAY, BUDDY.
UNGH.
THAP!

GOOD SAVE.
RU- UNGH.
OKAY, LET'S DO THIS.
THCK!
THUNK!
SPLAK!
WE'RE FINE! IT'S ALL UNDER CONTROL!

IF WE'RE NOT AT LEAST TWENTY MILES FROM ATLANTA NOW... WE'RE REALLY DAMN CLOSE. LET'S START LOOKING FOR SOME HOUSES OR NEIGHBORHOODS AND GET OFF THIS HIGHWAY.
WILL DO.
JESUS!! ARE WE EVEN GOING TO BE ABLE TO MOVE THIS MESS?
IT MIGHT TAKE A WHILE, BUT I THINK WE CAN.
WELL... LET'S GET STARTED... IT'S GOING TO BE DARK IN A FEW HOURS.

MAN, I'M GLAD WE RAN INTO YOU WHEN WE DID. EVEN WITH USING THE RV TO DO MOST OF THE PUSHING I DON'T THINK WE COULD HAVE CLEARED THAT WRECK OFF THE ROAD WITHOUT YOUR HELP.
I'M JUST TRYING TO PULL MY OWN WEIGHT, RICK. I'M GLAD YOU PEOPLE ARE LETTING US TAG ALONG.
WELL, SO FAR I GOTTA SAY... YOU'VE COME IN HANDY. ASIDE FROM RICK I DON'T THINK ANY OF US ARE REALLY ALL THAT STRONG.
I KNOW PUSHING CARS OUT OF THE WAY WAS A LOT HARDER BEFORE YOU CAME ALONG.
YOU'RE NOT TOO HARD ON THE EYES, EITHER.
RIGHT BACK AT YOU, CAROL.

YOU GUYS SURE DO HAVE A LOT OF FOOD.
WE'VE GOT GLENN TO THANK FOR THAT. BEFORE WE LEFT, WE'D BEEN STOCKPILING CANNED GOODS HE WAS GETTING FROM ATLANTA
I WAS JUST DOING MY PART.
OH, DON'T DOWNPLAY IT SO MUCH, GLENN... WITHOUT YOU WE'D BE MUCH WORSE OFF. WE'D HAVE TO RELY ON HUNTING WAY TOO MUCH.
YOU'RE A LIFESAVER.
I'VE GOT TO AGREE WITH THE LADY, GLENN.
I HAVEN'T EATEN THIS WELL IN WEEKS.

AS A GUY WHO'S SEEN HIM IN ACTION... I GOTTA SAY, GLENN REALLY KNEW WHAT HE WAS DOING IN THAT CITY.
THE FACT THAT HE RISKED HIS LIFE EVERY DAY FOR THE GOOD OF THE CAMP... THAT'S HONORABLE.
IF HE HADN'T BEEN THERE WHEN I FIRST GOT INTO ATLANTA... I PROBABLY WOULD HAVE NEVER FOUND LORI AND CARL... IF I EVEN SURVIVED.
I UH...
HOLD ON FOR A SECOND, GUYS.
LORI?

LORI!?
LORI, IS EVERYTHING OKAY?
NO, RICK.
I'M PREGNANT.

PREGNANT?
HOW LONG?
I DON'T KNOW... A WEEK... TWO. MY PERIODS HAVEN'T BEEN REGULAR SINCE THE BEGINNING. ALL THIS STRESS I SUPPOSE.
ARE YOU SURE?
I'M SURE. I KNOW EXACTLY WHAT IT FEELS LIKE. NO DOUBT IN MY MIND--
I'M PREGNANT.
WHAT ARE WE GOING TO DO?
I DON'T KNOW.
I'M ASKING YOU.

EVERYTHING OKAY?
I'M PREGNANT.
I JUST WANTED TO TELL RICK FIRST.
WE'RE GOING TO HAVE A BABY.
UM... WOW. I JUST--I DON'T KNOW WHAT TO SAY.
"CONGRATULATIONS" HAS WORKED FOR YEARS.
SORRY RICK... I'M JUST WORRIED. WE GOT NO DOCTORS, NO HOSPITAL. WHAT ARE YOU GOING TO DO?
WE'LL CROSS THAT BRIDGE WHEN WE COME TO IT.
WE'RE GOING TO BE FINE, ALLEN. THIS IS GOOD NEWS.

SHIT, IT'S STARTING TO SNOW. DID WE BOIL ENOUGH WATER TO FILL ALL THE BOTTLES WE HAVE?
JUST ABOUT, IT'S A GOOD THING WE FOUND THE CREEK WHEN WE DID.
RICK, ABOUT WHAT WE WERE TALKING ABOUT THE OTHER DAY... SHANE AND LORI... YOU DON'T THINK--?
LOOK, DALE... JUST DROP IT. OKAY?
IT'S JUST THAT YOU'VE ONLY BEEN WITH US A LITTLE OVER A MONTH. THE TIMING OF THIS COULD MEAN--
NOT ANOTHER WORD, DALE. NOT ANOTHER GODDAMN WORD!
I KNOW EXACTLY WHAT YOU'RE SAYING. YOU THINK I'M NOT THINKING ABOUT THAT? IT'S ALL I'M THINKING ABOUT. WE'VE ONLY HAD SEX ONCE SINCE I GOT BACK... I'M OUT OF MY MIND OVER THIS. BUT I TRUST MY WIFE, AND THAT'S ALL I CAN DO.
I'M TRYING NOT TO THINK ABOUT IT. IF I DWELL ON THIS I'LL LOSE MY MIND.
I'M WORRIED SICK AND ALLEN ISN'T HELPING A BIT. THIS COULD KILL LORI... AND I--THE OTHER THING COULD KILL ME.
I JUST CAN'T DEAL WITH THIS RIGHT NOW.
RICK. I-- I'M SORRY I BROUGHT IT UP.
DON'T WORRY, SON, EVERYTHING WILL WORK OUT. YOU DIDN'T SURVIVE THIS LONG JUST TO LOSE IT NOW.
ESPECIALLY IF YOU GOT A NEW BABY ON THE WAY.
C'MON... LET'S GET SOME SLEEP.

SHIT.
THIS PLACE WOULD HAVE BEEN PERFECT.
COME ON... LET'S GO.
THERE'S NOTHING FOR US HERE.

DON'T STRAY TOO FAR FROM THE RV, WE NEED TO BE BACK ON THE ROAD SOON.
UAUGH!!
OH GOD!
OH GOD!
OH GOD!
OH GOD!
DALE!

I--I WAS JUST WALKING ALONG. I DIDN'T EVEN SEE IT. SORRY TO STARTLE EVERYONE.
OH MY GOD, DALE! ARE YOU OKAY? DID IT HURT YOU?! ARE YOU OKAY?!
I'M FINE, ANDREA. I JUST FELL. I'M GOING TO BE JUST FINE.
WHAT'S GOING--?
OH HELL.
IS IT DEAD?
I THINK IT'S FROZEN.
UGG.
YEAAAA!!
WHOA. THAT PRETTY MUCH WHAT HAPPENED TO YOU?
YEAH, BUT IT'S FUNNIER TO WATCH, AND NOT AS PAINFUL.
KROK!
I GUESS THEY DON'T HAVE BLOOD PUMPING THROUGH THEM... SO THEY MUST FREEZE FASTER THAN US.
THAT'S GOOD TO KNOW.
WE SHOULD BE SAFE AS LONG AS THIS WEATHER KEEPS UP.

ARE WE OUT OF CANNED PEARS?
LAST TIME I CHECKED I DIDN'T SEE ANY. WE'VE GOT ABOUT THREE MORE CANS OF PEACHES THOUGH. OTHER THAN THAT, THE FRUIT IS ALMOST GONE.
CRAP... I REALLY LIKED THE PEARS. AND I HATE PEACHES.
ARE YOU WORRIED?
ABOUT THE BABY, I MEAN.
YEAH, OF COURSE. I MEAN... PEOPLE HAVE BEEN GIVING BIRTH UNASSISTED FOR CENTURIES BUT IT DOESN'T MAKE THE THOUGHT OF IT ANY EASIER.
NOT BEING ABLE TO GET CHECKED OUT AND MAKE SURE EVERYTHING IS OKAY ISN'T TOO DESIRABLE EITHER. I COULD BE HAVING TWINS AND NOT EVEN KNOW IT.
AND MORPHINE. YOU'RE NOT GOING TO HAVE ANY MORPHINE.
SHIT. I HADN'T THOUGHT OF THAT.
AW, MOM! YOU SAID A BAD WORD. YOU OWE ME A QUARTER!
TEE HEE!
OH, CARL. PUT IT ON MY TAB.
OVER THERE! STOP! PULL OVER!
I SEE IT!

I THINK WE'VE HIT THE JACKPOT.

WE'RE AT LEAST TWENTY MILES FROM THE CITY... WE SHOULD BE RELATIVELY SAFE HERE.
MY GOD. IF THE SNOW HADN'T HAD US GOING TEN MILES AN HOUR WE MIGHT HAVE MISSED THIS PLACE.
THIS PLACE IS PERFECT. WE COULD START A NEW LIFE HERE.
IT DOES LOOK PROMISING.
OKAY, LET'S ALL HAVE A LOOK AROUND BUT DON'T SPREAD TOO FAR APART. LET'S JUST CHECK OUT THESE FIRST FEW HOUSES FOR TODAY. WE DON'T KNOW JUST HOW ABANDONED THIS PLACE REALLY IS AND IT'S GOING TO BE DARK SOON, SO STAY SHARP.
BOYS, YOU STAY WITH CAROL, OKAY?
I'M GOING TO TAKE THE KIDS BACK INTO THE RV UNTIL YOU GUYS GIVE THE ALL CLEAR.
SOUNDS GOOD.
PROBABLY NOT A BAD IDEA TO KEEP YOUR GUNS OUT, EVERYONE.

SO FAR SO GOOD.
OH, AND THEY'VE GOT SUCH BIG YARDS.
THIS PLACE LOOKS PRETTY DESERTED.
I DON'T KNOW WHEN ANDREA IS GOING TO SNAP OUT OF IT. THE WAY SHE JUST SITS AROUND MOPING ALL DAY, YOU'D THINK SHE'D BEEN BITTEN.
I'M WORRIED ABOUT HER.
THIS HOUSE IS EMPTY.
WHAT ABOUT YOU GUYS? ALL CLEAR?
FAR AS WE CAN TELL. I DON'T SEE ANYTHING ANYWHERE NEAR THIS AREA.
GOOD. I DON'T KNOW ABOUT YOU GUYS, BUT I REALLY DON'T WANT TO SPEND ANOTHER NIGHT PACKED INTO THAT RV. WHAT DO YOU GUYS SAY TO GRABBING ALL OUR BLANKETS AND CRASHING IN ONE OF THESE HOUSES TONIGHT?
THE WINDOWS ON THE SECOND FLOOR OF THIS ONE SEEM TO BE FINE. WE SHOULD BE PRETTY WARM UP THERE. TOMORROW WE CAN START CLEARING OUT THE HOUSES AND GIVING PEOPLE THEIR OWN LIVING SPACE.
SOUNDS LIKE A PLAN TO ME.
ALL RIGHT THEN, LET'S ROUND UP THE OTHERS AND GET SETTLED IN.

TYREESE AND I ARE GOING TO CHECK OUT THE REST OF THE HOUSE. EVERYONE STAY HERE UNTIL WE GET BACK.
I'LL LOOK AROUND UPSTAIRS.
YELL IF YOU SEE ANYTHING.
DEPENDING ON WHAT I SEE... I MIGHT NOT HAVE MUCH OF A CHOICE.
LOOKS LIKE THERE'S A BASEMENT! THESE HOUSES ARE BIGGER THAN THEY LOOK.

HUNGH!
YEEAGH!
SHIT!

SHIT!
SHIT!
SHIT!
SLUKK!
DAMMIT!
WHUMP!
OOF!
DALE?! GLENN?! A LITTLE HELP HERE?!
HOLD ON, RICK!
PUSH UP THEIR HEADS, I CAN'T GET A CLEAR SHOT!

FWUMP!

THUD!
I GOT YOUR BACK, MAN!

LET'S PASTE THESE SUCKERS!

BE HAPPY TO!

SHUNK!

WHAM! WHAM! WHAM! WHAM!

WHACK! WHACK!

WE GOOD?
FOR NOW.
WE GOTTA CLEAR OUT THAT BASEMENT. GLENN, GET YOUR FLASHLIGHT.
LISTEN UP, WE'LL PROBABLY HEAR SOMETHING DOWN HERE BEFORE WE SEE IT.
KAHHH.
TYREESE, WE GOT ONE.
I'M ON IT.
WHAM!
REST LOOKS ALL CLEAR.
UPSTAIRS LOOK OKAY?
YEAH, I WAS DOING A FINAL PASS WHEN I HEARD YOU SCREAM. LOOKS LIKE EVERYTHING BUT THE BASEMENT WAS CLEAN.

THAT WAS A HELL OF A SAVE IN THERE BY THE STAIRS. WHERE'D YOU LEARN TO TACKLE LIKE THAT?
NFL.
NO SHIT? YOU WERE A PRO FOOTBALL PLAYER?
YEAH, FOR TWO YEARS. THEN I WAS A BOUNCER FOR A WHILE, THEN ODD JOBS, AND EVENTUALLY I SETTLED INTO BEING A CAR SALESMAN. WHICH IS WHAT I DID FOR ABOUT FIVE YEARS UNTIL ALL THIS SHIT WENT DOWN.
YOU KNOW HOW PEOPLE SIT AROUND AND SAY: "EVEN THE LOWEST PAID PRO ATHLETES STILL MAKE A COUPLE HUNDRED GRAND A YEAR"? I WAS ONE OF THOSE GUYS.
THE PAY WAS GOOD, BUT I WANTED THE GLORY. I ENDED UP TRYING A LITTLE TOO HARD TO IMPRESS MY COACH AND I ENDED UP GETTING HURT.
STILL, THAT'S PRETTY IMPRESSIVE. SURE BEATS "SMALL TOWN COP."
I DON'T KNOW... I NEVER GOT TO CARRY A GUN.
WELL, I NEVER REALLY USED MINE, NOT BEFORE THE DEAD STOPPED DYING, ANYWAY.
REALLY? I HAD YOU PEGGED AS THE HERO COP, THE WAY YOU'VE BEEN HANDLING YOURSELF THE PAST FEW DAYS.
LORD, NO. I WAS A REGULAR BARNEY FIFE.
WELL, YOU'VE CERTAINLY STEPPED UP TO THE CHALLENGE.
WE SHOULD PROBABLY BURN THESE GUYS TOMORROW.

WE'LL PROBABLY FIND MORE WHEN WE SEARCH THE HOUSES TOMORROW. SO WE'LL BURN THEM WHEN WE'VE GOT A GOOD PILE. WE'RE ALMOST USED TO THE SMELL NOW-- WHICH MAKES ME SICK--SO WE CAN WAIT A DAY TO BURN THEM TO SAVE MATCHES.
THIS PLACE IS LOADED WITH CANNED GOODS.
THEY GOT PEARS?
PEARS, APPLES, PINEAPPLES, PEACHES, CHERRIES... IF THEY CANNED GRAPES I'M SURE THEY'D HAVE THEM TOO.
WITH STOCK LIKE THIS YOU'D THINK THEY KNEW WHAT WAS COMING.
THAT'S GOOD TO HEAR. WHEN I SAW THE BROKEN WINDOW I WAS WORRIED. BUT THE LOOTING MUST HAVE HAPPENED EARLY ON, BACK WHEN PEOPLE WERE STEALING TVS, VCRS AND COMPUTERS. EVERYONE MUST HAVE FLED TO ATLANTA BY THE TIME PEOPLE REALIZED CANNED GOODS WERE MORE VALUABLE.
LUCKY FOR US.
OKAY, IT'S GETTING LATE AND I'M ITCHING TO START SEARCHING THIS PLACE TOMORROW. I SAY WE HIT THE SACK. IT'D BE SAFER IF WE ALL SLEPT UPSTAIRS. AS LIGHT AS WE SLEEP NOW, WE'D ALL HEAR SOMETHING COMING UP THE STEPS AND I'M SURE IT'D ALSO SLOW THEM DOWN A GREAT DEAL.
THING IS, WE GOT FOUR ROOMS AND A BATHROOM UPSTAIRS. I KNOW SOME OF YOU WERE REALLY LOOKING TO HAVING SOME PLACES OFF WITH YOUR FAMILIES BUT FOR TONIGHT AT LEAST IT LOOKS LIKE WE'LL BE STILL BUNKING UP SOME. ANY VOLUNTEERS?
I'LL TAKE THE BATHROOM. I'VE SLEPT IN MY SHARE OF TUBS FROM MY COLLEGE YEARS. I'VE GOT NO PROBLEM WITH IT.
SOPHIA AND I COULD SHARE A ROOM WITH TYREESE, JULIE AND CHRIS.
HEH.
THAT TAKES CARE OF THAT. LET'S GET THE BLANKETS UPSTAIRS AND GET SOME REST.
THAP!

HE'S OUT. POOR THING... HE NEVER REALLY COULD SLEEP IN THE RV.
YEAH, THE RV WAS WARMER WITH ALL OF US CRAMMED IN THERE, BUT I DON'T THINK THERE WAS A COMFORTABLE PLACE TO SLEEP IN THE WHOLE DAMN THING. AND THE NOISE... JEEZ, THERE WAS ALWAYS SOMEONE ROLLING OVER, COUGHING, OR JUST WAKING UP FROM A NIGHTMARE.
AND THE SMELL... DON'T FORGET THE SMELL.
THAT THING DID GET PRETTY RIPE NEAR THE END. JESUS, I CAN'T BELIEVE WE'RE ACTUALLY GOING TO SLEEP IN A BED. I'D FORGOTTEN WHAT IT WAS LIKE.
WHAT ARE WE GOING TO DO, RICK?
WELL, I FIGURE I'VE GOT ABOUT EIGHT MONTHS TO FIND YOU A DOCTOR. ONCE WE GET SETTLED IN HERE I GUESS I'LL GO OUT ON THE ROAD.
YOU ALWAYS WANTED TO HAVE ANOTHER KID BEFORE CARL GOT TOO OLD. I GUESS WHEN IT'S TIME IT'S TIME, Y'KNOW. STILL, THIS IS ONE MORE COMPLICATION WE DON'T NEED.
I KNOW, RICK. I'M WORRIED TOO, BUT NOW THAT WE'VE GOT THIS NEW PLACE... I AM FEELING A LITTLE BETTER ABOUT THE WHOLE THING.
IT'S JUST--
WE'LL GET THROUGH THIS, HON', DON'T WORRY.
I WAS POKING AROUND IN OUR CLOSET AND I FOUND SOME BLANKETS, YOU GUYS WANT AN EXTRA ONE?
SURE, DONNA THANKS.

GOOD NIGHT, GUYS.
OH, TYREESE... HEY. I FOUND SOME BLANKETS IN OUR CLOSET. THERE'S ENOUGH FOR EVERYONE TO HAVE ONE EXTRA.
TAKE THREE. GIVE ONE TO CAROL AND SOPHIA. AND CAN YOU SWING THE THIRD BY THE BATHROOM AND GIVE IT TO GLENN?
SURE. NO PROBLEM, DONNA AND THANKS.
HEY, TYREESE. I DON'T THINK I'VE GOTTEN A CHANCE TO WELCOME YOU TO OUR GROUP. I'M REALLY GLAD YOU'VE DECIDED TO STICK AROUND. YOU'VE REALLY BEEN A BIG HELP, AND JULIE IS THE SWEETEST LITTLE GIRL.
WELL THAT'S NICE OF YOU TO SAY. WE'RE REALLY LUCKY TO HAVE FOUND SUCH NICE PEOPLE. ESPECIALLY WHEN WE DID... WE WERE OUT OF FOOD, WITH NO SHELTER... WE PROBABLY WOULDN'T HAVE MADE IT IF WE HADN'T RAN INTO YOU THAT NIGHT.
I REALLY APPRECIATE ALL YOU PEOPLE HAVE GIVEN US. YOU CAN ALWAYS COUNT ON ME TO DO MY PART AROUND HERE.
GOODNIGHT, DONNA.
GOODNIGHT, TYREESE. SLEEP WELL.
DALE?
ANDREA?
GUYS, I FOUND--

...
click.

ANDREA'S FINE.
HUH? WHAT?
I WENT IN THERE TO GIVE THEM A BLANKET AND I SAW THEM... ALMOST ALL OF THEM... TOGETHER. SO WE'RE GETTING THEIR EXTRA BLANKET.
I DIDN'T WANT TO INTERRUPT.
REALLY? WOW. LUCKY FOR US THEN, HUH?
I FIGURED THEY DIDN'T NEED IT... THEY'RE KEEPING EACH OTHER PLENTY WARM.
Y'KNOW... I STILL DON'T APPROVE OF THOSE TWO, BUT ANDREA'S A GROWN WOMAN AND SHE CAN MAKE HER OWN DECISIONS. IT'S JUST NICE TO SEE PEOPLE HAPPY WITH ALL THAT'S GOING ON.
I'M HAPPY FOR THEM.
THE ICE QUEEN MELTETH.
OH, HUSH.
SPEAKING OF WHICH, I THINK IT'S WARMING UP A LITTLE OUTSIDE. THE SNOW IS MELTING OFF THE WINDOW.

SHIRE ESTATES
PLOP
PLOP
PLOP
PLOP
ALL DEAD
DO NOT
ENTER

LORI!?
LORI!?

SHHH
YOU'LL WAKE HIM UP.
OH, SORRY. HOW LONG HAVE YOU BEEN UP?
A FEW MINUTES... A HALF HOUR, I WASN'T REALLY KEEPING TRACK. NOT TOO LONG.
LOOK AT HIM, SO PEACEFUL. HE HASN'T SLEPT LIKE THIS SINCE WE LEFT HARRISON COUNTY.
I CAN'T IMAGINE HOW HARD ALL THIS HAS BEEN ON HIM, SHANE--JIM AND AMY... ALL OF IT. HELL, LORI... I DON'T KNOW HOW I'M COPING WITH IT.
THAT'S WHAT I'VE BEEN THINKING ABOUT. THIS NEW BABY WILL NEVER KNOW WHAT THE WORLD WAS LIKE, HELL... CARL WON'T REALLY REMEMBER MUCH OF IT HIMSELF BEFORE TOO LONG.
HE'LL NEVER KNOW WHAT IT'S LIKE TO GET HIS DRIVER'S LICENSE, OR GO SEE A MOVIE WITH A GIRL.
RICK, DO YOU THINK WE'LL EVER BE ABLE TO FIX EVERYTHING?
I DON'T KNOW.
I HOPE SO.

I... UM... SORRY. I GUESS I--IN MY SLEEP... UH.
NO, TYREESE... IT'S OKAY. REALLY.
I LIKE IT.

WHAT ARE YOU THINKING?
I DIDN'T KNOW YOU WERE AWAKE.
SURPRISE.
I WAS JUST THINKING ABOUT ANDREA AND DALE... THEY BOTH LOST SOMEONE THEY LOVED... SOMEONE VERY CLOSE TO THEM. IT HIT THEM HARD, WE SAW THAT... BUT THEY EVENTUALLY PULLED OUT OF IT. SEEING THEM TOGETHER LAST NIGHT-- THEY'RE HAPPY.
SEEING THEM--KNOWING THAT THEY CAN PUT THEIR LIVES BACK TOGETHER... IT GIVES ME HOPE.
AND THEN THERE'S THIS PLACE... A CHANCE TO START OVER. A NEW PLACE... ALL TO OURSELVES, AND IF HALF OF THE HOUSES IN THIS NEIGHBORHOOD ARE A NICE AS THIS ONE WE'LL ALL BE HAPPY. THIS PLACE--IT'S PERFECT.
I THINK WE CAN BE HAPPY HERE.
...AND EVERYONE WE'RE WITH. THEY'RE GOOD PEOPLE. I CAN'T BELIEVE WE STUMBLED INTO FINDING PEOPLE LIKE THEM. WE COULDN'T ASK FOR BETTER NEIGHBORS.
WE'RE REALLY LUCKY.
YOU'RE RIGHT. IF THIS WORKS OUT WE'VE GOT IT MADE. IT'S BEEN A WHILE SINCE I'VE SEEN YOU THIS HAPPY, DONNA.
YOU WANT TO HAVE SEX?
WHAT'S A SEGS?
THAT ANSWER YOUR QUESTION?

MORNING, EVERYONE. TODAY'S THE FUN PART. WE'RE GOING TO SPLIT INTO GROUPS AND SEARCH THROUGH ALL THESE HOUSES--OR AS MANY AS WE CAN.
WE'RE LOOKING FOR CANNED GOODS, AND SUPPLIES, FIRST AID KITS, AND MORE IMPORTANTLY... MAKING SURE THIS PLACE IS SECURE AND THAT THERE AREN'T ANY HOUSEGUESTS HIDING INSIDE LIKE THERE WERE WITH THIS ONE.
KEEP YOUR GUNS OUT AND BE READY TO FIRE. THIS IS GOING TO BE DANGEROUS SO KEEP YOUR EYES OPEN AND STAY ALERT.
ALSO, KEEP IN MIND THAT WE'LL ALL BE SPREADING OUT INTO THESE HOUSES AFTER WE SECURE THEM, SO LOOK THEM OVER, IF YOU SEE ONE YOU LIKE... KEEP IT IN MIND. LOOKS LIKE THERE'S GOING TO BE MORE THAN ENOUGH TO GO AROUND.
DAD, CAN CHRIS AND I STAY HERE? WE'RE SCARED. WE DON'T WANT TO GO SEARCHING THROUGH DARK HOUSES.
PLEASE?
THAT'S FINE. THEY CAN STAY HERE WITH ANDREA AND THE KIDS. IT'S NOT A BIG DEAL. THEY DON'T REALLY KNOW HOW TO USE GUNS YET ANYHOW.
DONNA, ALLEN, TYREESE, AND CAROL WILL BE ONE SEARCH TEAM. MYSELF, LORI, GLENN, AND DALE WILL BE THE OTHER. SOUND GOOD?
OKAY. I'M GOING TO GO GET TYREESE A GUN OUT OF THE RV.

MY TEAM, LET'S START ACROSS THE STREET. TYREESE, YOUR CREW WILL TAKE NEXT DOOR. I'LL BE RIGHT BACK WITH THAT GUN.
SWEEP THE YARDS REAL QUICK. JUST GIVE THEM A ONCE OVER BEFORE WE GO IN THE HOUSES.
THIS IS GOING TO BE SO FUN... LIKE ONE OF THOSE HOME SHOWS BUT BETTER.
YEAH, ASSUMING THESE HOUSES ARE ALL EMPTY.
CAROL AND I ARE GOING TO CHECK THE BACKYARD. SHOULDN'T TAKE A SECOND.
OKAY. WE'LL GO CHECK AROUND BY THE GARAGE.
ACTUALLY. I'M GOING TO GET A PEEK INSIDE.
BE CAREFUL, HON'. DON'T GO ALL THE WAY IN YET. JUST LOOK IN THE WINDOWS OR SOMETHING. WAIT UNTIL TYREESE HAS HIS GUN AND WE CAN ALL GO IN.
YOU WORRY TOO MUCH.

ALL DEAD
DO NOT
ENTER
WHAT?
ALL DEAD
DO NOT
ENTER
OH, FUCK.

AAHHH!!
HMMGG!
AHHGGG!!
ACK!
...
DONNA!
OH, GOD!

DON'T SHOOT!! DON'T FIRE YOUR GUNS!!
WHATEVER YOU DO, DON'T SHOOT!
GET AWAY FROM HER!!
ALLEN, NO! THERE'S NOTHING YOU CAN DO FOR HER NOW! YOU'LL JUST GET YOURSELF KILLED!
NGH
BLAM!
NOOO!

WE NEED TO GET OUT OF HERE. NOW.
WHAT? WHAT DO YOU MEAN? IS SOMETHING GOING ON?
YES. WE NEED TO BE IN THE RV AND OUT OF HERE RIGHT NOW.
OH, SHIT!
GO! GET EVERYONE INTO THE RV. I'LL GET ALLEN.
ALLEN! WE NEED TO GO NOW!
NO. I CAN'T-- NOT WITHOUT HER. JUST LEAVE ME RICK.
LEAVE ME HERE.
NO, GODDAMMIT!! THINK OF YOUR KIDS, ALLEN! THEY NEED A FATHER! THEY NEED YOU! NOW MORE THAN EVER!
I WON'T LEAVE YOU HERE.

IF WE DON'T GO NOW WE'RE BOTH DEAD!
BLAM!
C'MON!
DALE! GET THE RV STARTED! WE'VE GOT TO GET OUT OF HERE IN A HURRY!!
YOU GUYS, HELP US GET THE KIDS!
FOLLOW ME!
OH, GOD!
WAS THAT GUNFIRE?
GET THE KIDS! WE'RE LEAVING!
WHERE ARE JULIE AND CHRIS?!
OH, SHIT! THEY WENT UPSTAIRS.
I'LL GET THEM! YOU GO TO THE RV!

WHERE'S DONNA?
DEAD. WHERE'S TYREESE?
OH GOD. I--HE--HE HAD TO GO BACK FOR JULIE AND CHRIS.
SHIT! IF THE ZOMBIES GET CLOSE TO THE RV, DRIVE OFF! WE'LL FIGHT OUR WAY OUT! DON'T WORRY ABOUT US!
RICK!
DAMN.
DAMN.
DAMN.
BLAM!
BLAM!
SHIT!

WHAT THE FUCK ARE YOU DOING?!
I'M SORRY, DADDY! WE JUST--
WE DON'T HAVE TIME FOR THIS! GET YOUR GODDAMN CLOTHES ON!
YOU GOT 'EM? GOOD. WE CAN'T GET OUT THAT WAY. ANY IDEAS?
SLAM!
WINDOW!

OKAY... WHAT THE HELL ARE WE GOING TO DO NOW?
LOOK!
WHAM!
JUMP ON THE ROOF!
HOLD ON TIGHT!
WE'RE ON! LET'S GO!
CHOOM!

WHERE'S MOMMY?
SHE'S-- YOUR MOTHER HAS--I--
SHE'S DEAD! YOUR MOTHER IS DEAD!

I'M SORRY, ALLEN. I JUST DON'T KNOW WHAT TO SAY.
THEN DON'T SAY ANYTHING. JUST LEAVE ME ALONE.
I'M JUST WORRIED ABOUT HIM.
WHAT GOOD IS THAT GOING TO DO? THE ONLY THING WE CAN DO TO "FIX" ALLEN IS TO BRING BACK HIS WIFE... AND WE CAN'T DO THAT.
JUST LET HIM MOURN--FOR AS LONG AS IT TAKES. YOU DON'T KNOW WHAT IT'S LIKE TO LOSE A SPOUSE, RICK. HE'S GOING THROUGH HELL RIGHT NOW. I KNOW.
THERE'S NO GREEN BEANS...THERE'S NO CORN. HELL... WE'RE ALMOST OUT OF EVERYTHING.
IF ONLY WE COULD HAVE GRABBED THE CANNED FOOD OUT OF THAT HOUSE BEFORE WE LEFT.
JESUS... WHAT ARE WE GOING TO DO?

BE CAREFUL GUYS... BE READY FOR ANYTHING.
WHO KNOWS... SHIT. THIS IS NOT GOOD.
DAMN.
ANYTHING THAT WASN'T TAKEN WAS DESTROYED. WHY THE HELL WOULD ANYONE DO THIS?
HOW THE HELL ARE WE GOING TO MAKE IT WITHOUT ANY FOOD?
I SEE LOTS OF HUNTING IN OUR FUTURE.

WE SHOULDN'T BE OUT TOO LONG. EVEN IF WE DON'T FIND ANYTHING WE'LL BE BACK BEFORE IT GETS DARK.
IF YOU SEE ANYTHING, FIRE A SHOT, WE'LL BE BACK HERE AS SOON AS WE CAN.
WE'LL BE FINE. AS LONG AS YOU GO GET US SOMETHING TO EAT.
I'LL SEE WHAT I CAN DO.
CAN I COME TOO? I CAN HELP. I SHOOT REAL GOOD.
I KNOW. YOU CAN COME WITH US, BUT DON'T SHOOT UNLESS I TELL YOU TO. IT'S VERY IMPORTANT THAT IF WE DO FIND SOMETHING YOU DON'T SCARE IT OFF.
ALL RIGHT, WE'RE GOING. KEEP AN EYE ON ALLEN WHILE WE'RE GONE. OKAY, HON'?
OKAY, DAD.
WHO KNOWS WHAT'S GOING THROUGH HIS HEAD RIGHT NOW.
I'M AFRAID HE MAY HURT HIMSELF... OR WORSE.

DO YOU REALLY THINK ALLEN MIGHT HURT HIMSELF?
HE WANTED ME TO LEAVE HIM FOR DEAD BACK AT THOSE HOUSES A WEEK AGO. I DON'T KNOW WHAT THE MAN'S GOING THROUGH... I DON'T KNOW WHAT HE'S CAPABLE OF.
I DON'T THINK HE COULD HURT ANYONE ELSE. ALLEN IS A GOOD FATHER, AND AN ALL AROUND GREAT GUY. I DON'T THINK IT'LL GO THAT FAR.
I GOTTA SAY, THOUGH... AFTER WHAT HAPPENED WITH SHANE... I JUST DON'T KNOW ANYMORE.
YEAH, CAROL WAS TELLING ME ABOUT ALL THAT THE OTHER DAY.
SHHH!
DID YOU HEAR THAT?
I THINK THERE'S SOMETHING OUT THERE UP AHEAD OF US.

PKOW!
CARL! NO!
NO!
NO SON NO!
WHAT THE HELL?!
WHO THE FUCK IS SHOOTING AT US?!
SHOW YOURSELF!
PLEASE DON'T SHOOT ME.
IT WAS AN ACCIDENT, I SW-- SWEAR.

WHAT DID YOU DO?!
RICK!
I--
WHAT DID YOU DO?!
I'M SORRY, MISTER--I'M REALLY SORRY. I THOUGH YOU WAS ALL--
SORRY?!
DO YOU REALIZE WHAT YOU'VE DONE?!

I'LL KILL YOU!
I'LL FUCKING KILL YOU!

RICK! STOP!
DON'T DO IT!
HE'S STILL BREATHING, RICK!
CARL'S NOT DEAD!
HE'S... ALIVE?
HE'S ALIVE?

HE'S BREATHING?! HE'S ALIVE?!
WHAT DO WE DO? WHAT THE HELL DO WE DO? WE'VE GOTTA-- WHAT THE HELL DO WE DO?
HE'S BREATHING BUT HE'S UNCONSCIOUS... HE'S LOST A LOT OF BLOOD. WE'VE GOT TO DO SOMETHING TO STOP THE BLEEDING.
THERE'S GOT TO BE SOMETHING WE COULD DO!
YEAH, WE'VE GOT TO STOP THE BLEEDING. THERE'S A FIRST AID KIT AT THE RV. WE NEED TO GET HIM BACK TO THE RV.
I--AT THE FARM I LIVE ON... THE GUY THAT OWNS THE PLACE HAD A SON SHOT IN THE FOOT.
HE GOT THE BULLET OUT, PATCHED HIM UP GOOD. HE WORKS ON ANIMALS AROUND THE FARM.
YOU THINK HE COULD HELP MY SON?
HE AIN'T NO DOCTOR BUT I THINK HE'LL KNOW WHAT TO DO.
THE PLACE AIN'T A MILE AWAY... WE'D BE THERE RIGHT QUICK.

LESS THAN A MILE? I--I CAN DO THAT. TYREESE--GET READY TO HELP ME ROLL HIM OVER ONTO MY COAT.
OKAY, SLOWLY.
I'M GOING TO THIS FARM. YOU GO BACK TO THE RV AND TELL EVERYONE WHAT HAPPENED. IF IT'S LESS THAN A MILE FROM HERE YOU GUYS SHOULD BE ABLE TO FIND IT PRETTY EASILY.
IS IT PRETTY EASY TO FIND?
YOU CAN SEE IT FROM THE ROAD... IF Y'ALL ARE PARKED JUST UP YONDER YOU GOTTA BE ON SIXTY-FOUR. YOU'LL SNAKE AROUND THE ROAD AND IT'LL BE ON YOUR LEFT. IT'S A LITTLE FURTHER AWAY BY ROAD BUT YOU'LL FIND IT EASY.
C'MON, LET'S GO.
LEAD THE WAY, I'LL BE RIGHT BEHIND YOU.
TYREESE, TELL LORI THERE'S NOTHING TO WORRY ABOUT.
OKAY.

TYREESE!
WE HEARD THE SHOT, DID YOU GUYS GET SOMETHING? IS EVERYTHING O-- WHERE ARE THEY?
WHAT HAPPENED?! WHERE ARE THEY?!
SOME GUY THOUGHT WE WERE ZOMBIES... HE SHOT AT US! CARL WAS HIT BUT HE'S OKAY, RICK AND THIS GUY ARE TAKING CARL BACK TO SOME FARM SO ANOTHER GUY CAN HELP HIM, HE'S OKAY THOUGH.... HE'S JUST... THEY'RE GOING TO--
WHERE?! WHERE ARE THEY AT?!
WHERE?!
IT'S UP THE ROAD FROM HERE! I KNOW THE WAY!
LET'S GO!

WHERE'S YOUR PA?
HE'S AT THE HOUSE. WHAT'S GOIN' ON, OTIS?
WHO IS THAT?
AIN'T NO TIME, RIGHT NOW.
WHAT HAPPENED? WHO'S THIS? WHAT'S GOING ON?
BOY'S BEEN SHOT. WE NEED YOU TO GIVE HIM A LOOK.
LET'S GET HIM INSIDE! WHERE'S HE BEEN SHOT? HOW BAD IS IT?

HELP ME GET THIS SHIRT OFF HIM, OTIS. I'VE GOT TO PULL THIS BULLET OUT.
RUN THAT OVER THE FIRE TO STERILIZE IT. AND HAND ME THAT BOTTLE OF ALCOHOL.
OKAY... I THINK I'VE GOT A HOLD OF IT--HOLD HIM DOWN.
RICK!
WHERE IS HE? WHERE'S CARL? IS HE OKAY?!

THIS GUY'S WORKING ON HIM. HE SEEMS TO KNOW WHAT HE'S DOING.
I THINK HE'S STOPPED THE BLEEDING, AT LEAST.
OH, RICK... WHAT ARE WE GOING TO DO?
I DON'T KNOW, LORI. I JUST DON'T KNOW.
I'VE GOT HIM PATCHED UP. I PULLED THE BULLET OUT OF HIM AND I STOPPED THE BLEEDING. HE WAS REAL LUCKY. THE BULLET LODGED IN HIS SHOULDER BLADE... MUST'VE COME IN AT EXACTLY THE RIGHT ANGLE.
HAD THE BULLET BEEN A LITTLE MORE DETERMINED, IT COULD HAVE GONE RIGHT INTO HIS LUNG... HAD THAT HAPPENED... I WOULDN'T HAVE BEEN ABLE TO DO A WHOLE LOT OF ANYTHING FOR HIM.
HE'S STILL OUT... BUT I THINK HE'LL BE OKAY. ALL WE CAN DO AT THIS POINT IS JUST WAIT AND SEE.
THANKS, MISTER, I REALLY--
NAME'S HERSHEL GREENE. DON'T THANK ME JUST YET. YOUR TIME WOULD BE BETTER PUT TO USE PRAYING FOR THE BOY.
I AIN'T HAD A PRAYER ANSWERED IN A GOOD SOLID FEW MONTHS... SO I FIGURE WE'RE ABOUT DUE FOR SOMETHING GOOD.

I'M HERSHEL. THIS IS MY FARM. YOU GUYS ARE WELCOME TO STAY HERE WHILE THE BOY GETS BETTER. WE GOT PLENTY OF FOOD HARVESTED--BECAUSE WELL, THE MARKETS CLOSED--AND REALLY PLENTY OF ROOM. SO YOU'RE ALL WELCOME TO STAY FOR THE TIME BEING.
NOW, LET ME INTRODUCE YOU TO THE FOLKS LIVING HERE.
THIS IS LACEY, MY ELDEST DAUGHTER.
THE ONE WITH THE CHIP ON HIS SHOULDER IS MY SON ARNOLD.
MY DAUGHTER MAGGIE'S THE ONE HOLDING THAT CHAIR DOWN.
MY YOUNGEST SON, BILLY.
RACHEL AND SUSIE HERE ROUND OUT THE PACK. SUSIE'S THE ONE WITH THE PIGTAILS

THIS IS OTIS AND HIS GIRLFRIEND PATRICIA. THEY LIVE UP THE ROAD FROM HERE. OUR PLACE IS SAFER THAN THEIR PLACE SO THEY'RE STAYING WITH US UNTIL THIS WHOLE THING BLOWS OVER.
THAT'S ABOUT IT FOR US HERE, ASIDE FROM SOME CRITTERS RUNNING AROUND OUTSIDE.
LACEY, COULD YOU TAKE THEM OUT AND SHOW THEM AROUND THE FARM--LET THEM GET ACQUAINTED WITH THE PLACE? I WANT TO CHECK IN ON THE BOY, MAKE SURE EVERYTHING'S OKAY.
SURE. WHATEVER.
THIS IS OUR YARD... IF YOU'LL FOLLOW ME AROUND BACK I'LL SHOW YOU OUR BACKYARD.
I--UH... BILLY, BEN, AND I ARE GOING TO SIT THIS ONE OUT.
I'M JUST NOT UP TO IT.
THEY CAN STILL COME. I'LL KEEP AN EYE ON THEM, ALLEN. I'M SURE THEY'LL WANNA SEE THE COWS.
THAT'S FINE. GO WITH ANDREA, BOYS.
YEAH! I WANNA SEE COWS!

HE LOOKS SO PEACEFUL... SO CONTENT. I HOPE HE'S HAVING WONDERFUL DREAMS AND ENJOYING HIS BREAK FROM ALL THE MADNESS GOING ON OUT HERE.
IF ONLY HE COULD SLEEP UNTIL ALL THIS WAS OVER.
JESUS, RICK! WE DON'T WANT HIM TO BE IN A COMA!
WHAT A TERRIBLE THING TO SAY!
THAT'S NOT WHAT I MEANT... I-- DAMMIT! I JUST WISH THAT HE DIDN'T HAVE TO GO THROUGH ALL THIS SHIT WITH US.
IS THAT SO WRONG?
I--OH GOD, LORI... I'M SO DAMN WORRIED ABOUT HIM.
I LOVE YOU, LORI. I DON'T KNOW IF I SAY IT ENOUGH WITH ALL THAT'S GOING ON. I REALLY LOVE YOU. I'VE ALWAYS LOVED YOU.
I DON'T KNOW HOW I'D GET THROUGH ANY OF THIS WITHOUT YOU.
I LOVE YOU, TOO.
I LOVE YOU SO MUCH.

OTIS, RIGHT?
YEAH.
I DON'T KNOW IF YOU CAUGHT IT BEFORE, I'M TYREESE.
YOU DOING OKAY?
I WOULDN'T HURT A FLY--I MEAN... I WAS OUT THERE HUNTIN' BUT I WOULDN'T KILL NO ANIMAL I WASN'T GOING TO EAT. I'M REAL GENTLE, I AIN'T VIOLENT AT ALL.
AND I--I SHOT THAT KID. I UNDERSTAND WHY THAT RICK FELLA WANTED TO KILL ME. IF'N I HAD KILLED HIS BOY... I'D A WANTED HIM TO DO IT... I'D A DESERVED IT.
WE STILL DON'T KNOW IF HE'S GONNA LIVE.
I AIN'T SAYING WHAT YOU DID WAS RIGHT, BUT YOU CAN'T WORRY YOURSELF TO DEATH OVER IT. WHAT'S DONE IS DONE. I'M WORRIED SICK ABOUT CARL, BUT THERE'S NOTHING YOU OR I CAN DO ABOUT IT NOW.
HE SNAPPED.
RICK'S BEEN UNDER A LOT OF STRESS, WE ALL HAVE. WE JUST BARELY MADE IT OUT OF SOME NEIGHBORHOOD THAT WAS CRAWLING WITH THOSE ZOMBIES. OUR FRIEND LOST HIS WIFE THERE. THEN NOT A WEEK LATER HIS SON IS SHOT.
NEIGHBORHOOD? THAT MUST HAVE BEEN WILSHIRE ESTATES. PATRICIA AND I WERE THERE WHEN ALL THIS STARTED. EVERYONE IN THIS AREA WHO COULDN'T MAKE IT TO ATLANTA DECIDED TO HOLE UP THERE.
IT WAS A DISASTER... WE DIDN'T HAVE NO PROTECTION... ONCE THEM THINGS COME IN WE HAD NO WAY A STOPPING THEM. PATRICIA AND I BARELY MADE IT OUT ALIVE.
WE DIDN'T HAVE THE NATIONAL GUARD PROTECTING US LIKE THEY DO IN ATLANTA.
ACTUALLY, FROM WHAT EVERYONE IS SAYING... ATLANTA IS WORSE OFF.
REALLY? PATRICIA AND I WERE GOING TO TRY AND MAKE IT THERE WHEN SUMMER CAME... WE FIGURED IT'D BE SAFER THERE.
DAMN.

FWOP!
HEY, KIDS. GO PLAY WITH YOUR AUNT CAROL AND SOPHIA. YOUR DADDY AND I NEED TO TALK.
'KAY!
ALLEN, WE NEED TO TALK.
HUH? WHAT DO YOU WANT?
I WANT YOU TO THINK ABOUT YOUR KIDS. YOU'VE GOT TO BE STRONG FOR THEM. I KNOW YOU'RE UPSET, AND YOU HAVE EVERY RIGHT TO BE, BUT THOSE BOYS NEED YOU.
YOU CAN'T JUST SHUT DOWN LIKE THIS.
WHAT? WHAT THE HELL ARE YOU TELLING ME? GET OVER IT? STOP BEING SAD? YOU WANNA THROW "QUIT BEING A PUSSY" IN THERE TOO AND GO FOR THE HOME RUN?
I JUST LOST MY FUCKING WIFE YOU LITTLE CUNT. WHERE THE HELL DO YOU GET OFF TELLING ME ANYTHING ABOUT MY GRIEVING PROCESS?!
FUCK YOU!

WHAT? I DON'T KNOW WHAT IT'S LIKE TO LOSE SOMEONE?! I JUST LOST MY FUCKING SISTER! I THINK I KNOW A LITTLE ABOUT THE GRIEVING PROCESS. I KNOW EXACTLY WHAT YOU'RE GOING THROUGH! I SHUT DOWN WHEN I LOST AMY. I DIDN'T SPEAK FOR DAYS... I COULDN'T THINK... I ALMOST LOST MY MIND.
YOU DON'T HAVE THAT LUXURY. BEN AND BILLY NEED THEIR FATHER RIGHT NOW! I WAS JUST TRYING TO HELP YOU, ASSHOLE.
MY WIFE JUST DIED!
AND MY SISTER DIED, AND SHANE DIED, AND JIM DIED! MY PARENTS ARE PROBABLY DEAD! EVERYONE I'VE EVER KNOWN ARE PROBABLY DEAD!
MY FRIENDS, MY FAMILY, MY NEIGHBORS, MY CO-WORKERS... EVERYONE.
EVERYONE IN THIS GROUP IS DEALING WITH THAT... WE'RE SURROUNDED BY DEATH. IT'S TAKEN OVER OUR LIVES. AND THERE ISN'T A GODDAMN THING WE CAN DO ABOUT IT!
WE EITHER DEAL WITH IT OR WE DON'T AND RIGHT NOW YOUR SONS NEED YOU TO DEAL WITH IT... AND GET OVER IT.
THEY NEED YOU! THINK ABOUT THEM!
YOU LITTLE BITCH. DON'T COME OVER HERE AND TRY AND GIVE ME ADVICE. YOU DON'T KNOW SHIT. YOU'RE NOT HELPING ONE BIT.
ALL I CAN DO IS THINK ABOUT THEM! IT'S ALL I'VE DONE NOW FOR DAYS! I THINK ABOUT THEM GROWING UP WITHOUT THEIR MOTHER... I THINK ABOUT THEM GETTING OLDER... FORGETTING ABOUT HER... NOT EVEN REMEMBERING HER FACE.
I'M THINKING ABOUT THAT AND IT'S TEARING ME APART!
LEAVE ME THE FUCK ALONE!

YOUR SON IS AWAKE.
OH, THANK GOD!
WHERE'S MY HAT?
OH, SON. I'M SO GLAD YOU'RE AWAKE.
HOW ARE YOU FEELING, CARL? DOES IT STILL HURT?
MY SHOULDER DOES... BAD.
DON'T WORRY, SON. YOU'RE GOING TO BE OKAY.
NOBODY BETTER NOT'VE TAKEN MY HAT!

DON'T WORRY, KIDDO. I WAS KEEPING IT WARM FOR YOU.
DON'T MENTION IT. I'M JUST GLAD TO SEE THAT YOU'RE OKAY.
THANKS, TYREESE.
I GOTTA SAY, RICK. OTIS IS REALLY TORN UP ABOUT ALL THIS. IF YOU COULD JUST--I MEAN, HE SEEMS LIKE SUCH A NICE GUY...
WHAT AM I SUPPOSED TO SAY? "IT'S OKAY YOU SHOT MY SON?" IT'S NOT OKAY... I CAN'T JUST LET IT GO. WHAT HE DID WAS DAMN IRRESPONSIBLE.
IF HE'S THAT CARELESS HE SHOULDN'T BE ROAMING AROUND THE WOODS WITH A GUN IN THE FIRST PLACE.
I JUST DON'T SEE THE HARM IN--
SOMEBODY SHOT ME?
WHO SHOT ME?
OH, SON... I'M SORRY. IN THE WOODS, A MAN NAMED OTIS, HE ACCIDENTALLY SHOT YOU.
BUT DON'T WORRY, HONEY. EVERYTHING'S GOING TO BE OKAY NOW. YOU'RE GOING TO BE FINE.
OTIS HELPED ME TAKE YOU HERE, AND HIS FRIEND HERSHEL PATCHED YOU UP. WE'RE GOING TO BE STAYING HERE WHILE YOU REST... YOU'VE GOT A LOT OF NEW PEOPLE TO MEET, SON.
COOL. I LIKE MEETING NEW PEOPLE.

YOU MIND A LITTLE COMPANY? SOPHIA WANTS TO SEE CARL.
COME ON IN, LORI AND I WERE ABOUT TO GET SOMETHING TO EAT. I'M SURE HE WOULD LOVE THE COMPANY.
BE GOOD, CARL. GET SOME REST AFTER SOPHIA AND CAROL LEAVE.
LOOK AT THEM...
THEY LOOK SO CUTE TOGETHER.
LET'S LET THEM TALK.
DID IT HURT?
I DON'T KNOW... I DON'T REMEMBER. I THINK SO. I BET I'M GOING TO HAVE A BIG SCAR!
COOL. SCARS ARE SEXY.
SEXY? YOU DON'T EVEN KNOW WHAT THAT MEANS.
NEITHER DO YOU!
SO. I'M NOT THE ONE THAT TRIED TO SAY IT.
IT'S THE GROWN UP WORD FOR PRETTY... I THINK.
WELL... SCARS AREN'T PRETTY.
I'M GLAD YOU'RE OKAY.
SMECK!
EWWW! GROSS!

LORI?
WHAT CAN I DO FOR YOU, DALE?
I'M GOING TO TALK, AND YOU'RE GOING TO LISTEN. I'M AN OLD MAN... TOO OLD FOR ARGUMENTS. SO I WANT YOU TO KNOW THAT I REALLY DON'T WANT THIS TO BECOME ONE. I'M GOING TO SAY WHAT I HAVE TO SAY AND THEN WE'RE DONE.
RICK IS THE BACKBONE OF THIS GROUP. HE'S THE ONE STABLE THING WE'VE ALL GOT. HE KNOWS THIS. THAT'S WHY WHEN HE'S SCARED YOU CAN'T TELL... YOU KNOW HE'S SCARED, BUT HE AIN'T SHOWING IT. WE NEED THAT. WE NEED HIM.
I DON'T KNOW WHAT YOU DID WITH SHANE. I DON'T KNOW WHAT YOU DID TO PUT IDEAS IN HIS HEAD, BUT IF THAT BABY'S HIS... AND NOT RICK'S, I'M BEGGING YOU--TAKE IT TO YOUR GRAVE.
IT'LL KILL HIM. IT'LL BE THE ONE LAST THING IT TAKES TO MAKE HIM CRACK. AND WE DON'T NEED THAT.
I'M NOT ACCUSING YOU OF SHIT SO DON'T TRY TO DEFEND YOURSELF. I JUST WANTED TO SAY MY PIECE AND I APPRECIATE YOU SITTING THROUGH IT.
I THINK THEY'RE DONE WITH DINNER. LET'S GO EAT.

I'M IMPRESSED, HERSHEL. I'VE GOT TO SAY... YOU'VE REALLY GOT QUITE THE SET UP HERE.
I'M GOING TO TAKE CARL A PLATE BEFORE THE FOOD'S ALL GONE.
I THINK I KNOW HOW YOU FELT WHEN YOU FIRST RAN INTO US WITH ALL OUR CANNED GOODS, TYREESE.
GOTTA SAY, PAL... THIS GUY'S GOT ME A LITTLE BIT MORE IMPRESSED. AT THIS RATE, I THINK THE NEXT GUY I RUN INTO IS GOING TO HAVE A FOUR STAR RESTAURANT SET UP IN HIS MANSION.

GLENN, RIGHT? SO, UM... WHY YOU STARIN' AT THAT BLACK GUY'S GIRLFRIEND ALL THE TIME?
YOU DIDN'T TAKE YOUR EYES OFF HER ALL THROUGH DINNER.
HUH?
I SAW YOU LOOKING AT HER... WHAT'S UP WITH THAT?
BEFORE TYREESE CAME... I GUESS I HAD MY EYE ON CAROL... SHE'S A BIT OLDER THAN ME... BUT I LIKED HER.
I GUESS I'M JUST A LITTLE PISSED THAT I NEVER MADE MY MOVE.
YEAH, I GUESS SHE'S PRETTY.
IT'S NOT EVEN THAT... I MEAN... SHE IS PRETTY, BUT... I DON'T KNOW. EVERYONE AROUND ME IS PAIRING OFF. THERE'S JUST NOT THAT MANY WOMEN TO GO AROUND.
ON TOP OF ALL THAT'S GOING ON AROUND ME... I JUST DON'T WANT TO END UP ALONE TOO. I MEAN... I WANT TO HAVE SEX AT LEAST A COUPLE MORE TIMES BEFORE I DIE.
JESUS. I DON'T EVEN KNOW YOU. I'M SORRY. I DON'T MEAN TO SPILL MY GUTS LIKE THIS.
I'LL FUCK YOU.
IF THAT'S WHAT YOU'RE AFTER, I'LL FUCK YOU.
WHAT?
MY BOYFRIEND'S GONE-- PROBABLY DEAD. TO BE HONEST, HE WAS A BIT OF A JERK ANYWAY. YOU'RE THE FIRST GUY I'VE SEEN IN MONTHS THAT'S NOT RELATED TO ME OR THAT OTIS IDIOT. IT'S LIKE YOU SAID--OUR CHOICES AREN'T VERY BROAD.
WE'VE GOTTA BE PROACTIVE... OR WE'RE GOING TO END UP ALONE.
THAT DOES MAKE SENSE.
SO LET'S FUCK THEN. YOU WANNA DO THAT?
YEAH. SURE.

OKAY, GUYS. WE NEED TO TALK.
DAAAD!
DON'T "DAD" ME, YOUNG LADY. THIS ISN'T GOING TO GO ON RIGHT UNDER MY NOSE. I JUST DON'T HAVE TIME TO PUT UP WITH THIS.
I DON'T WANT TO HAVE TO WORRY ABOUT YOU TWO FOOLING AROUND ALL THE TIME. I DON'T WANT TO HAVE TO KEEP AN EYE ON YOU ON TOP OF ALL THE OTHER SHIT I'VE GOT TO DO.
YOU WANT TO GET PREGNANT? DO YOU NOT SEE HOW DANGEROUS THAT WOULD BE? I DON'T KNOW HOW RICK AND LORI ARE DEALING WITH IT THE WAY THEY ARE.
THIS ISN'T A GAME. I KNOW YOU TWO THINK YOU'RE IN LOVE BUT YOU'RE YOUNG... THINK ABOUT WHAT YOU'RE DOING.
SIGH
JUST KEEP YOUR HANDS TO YOURSELVES.
SEE? I TOLD YOU WE NEEDED TO GO AHEAD AND DO IT. I WANT TO BE TOGETHER WITH YOU FOR THE REST OF ETERNITY. I DON'T WANT YOUR FATHER TO STAND IN THE WAY OF THAT.
I KNOW... I JUST DON'T WANT TO DO IT UNTIL THE TIME IS RIGHT. WE HAVE TO WAIT.
FINE, JULIE. WE'LL PLAY IT YOUR WAY... BUT I DON'T WANT TO WAIT FOREVER.

MY DAD OWNED THIS PLACE. I GREW UP ON THIS FARM. BUT I NEVER LIKED IT. I WANTED TO BE A VETERINARIAN... SO THAT'S WHAT I DID. WORKING ON CREATURES GREAT AND SMALL WAS MY CALLING... AND I DID IT FOR YEARS.
AFTER MY WIFE DIED MY PRACTICE FELL APART... SHE ALWAYS HELD UP THE BUSINESS END... ALL I DID WAS WORK ON THE ANIMALS.
I COULDN'T DO MUCH OF ANYTHING WITHOUT HER.
SORRY TO HEAR ABOUT THAT. HOW LONG AGO WAS IT?
SHE PASSED ON ALMOST SIX YEARS AGO. IT WAS MY FATHER'S DYING WISH THAT I WOULD COME BACK AND WORK ON THE FARM.
IT JUST SEEMED LIKE THE RIGHT THING TO DO.
I'VE BEEN AT IT FOR FIVE YEARS NOW. IT'S HONEST WORK, I CAN SEE WHY MY DAD LOVED IT SO MUCH. THERE'S NOTHING QUITE LIKE LIVING OFF THE LAND... PROVIDING FOR YOURSELF... KNOWING EXACTLY WHERE EVERY PIECE OF FOOD YOU EAT COMES FROM.
IT'S CERTAINLY COME IN HANDY IN LIGHT OF CURRENT EVENTS.
THAT'S FOR SURE. SEEMS LIKE YOU'VE GOT A NICE, STABLE SET UP HERE.

YOU'RE WELCOME TO ENJOY IT WHILE CARL HEALS. I'D RECOMMEND STAYING HERE IN THAT TIME. IT WOULDN'T BE GOOD FOR HIM TO BE OUT IN THE ELEMENTS AGAIN... AT LEAST NOT RIGHT AWAY.
WE DON'T HAVE MUCH ROOM IN THE HOUSE, YOU'D STILL HAVE TO SLEEP IN YOUR RV, BUT WE GOT PLENTY OF FOOD AND DURING THE DAY YOU WON'T HAVE TO WORRY ABOUT BEING SAFE.
WHAT ABOUT YOUR BARN? YOU THINK WE COULD MOVE INTO THAT PLACE? MOST OF US ARE PRETTY SICK OF CRAMMING INTO THAT RV.
THE BARN? YOU DON'T WANT TO GO IN THERE, TRUST ME.
THAT'S WHERE WE KEEP ALL OUR DEAD ONES.

"DEAD ONES?!" WHAT DO YOU MEAN "DEAD ONES?"
YOU KNOW... THE DEAD ONES-- ALL THESE PEOPLE UP AND WALKING AROUND AFTER THEY SHOULDN'T BE. THE ONE'S THAT ARE CAUSING ALL THIS TROUBLE.
AND YOU'RE KEEPING THOSE... THINGS IN YOUR BARN--ON YOUR PROPERTY--RIGHT NEXT TO WHERE YOU SLEEP?
YEAH, WE'RE KEEPING THEM IN THE BARN UNTIL WE CAN FIGURE OUT A WAY TO HELP THEM. WHAT HAVE YOU BEEN DOING WITH THEM?
WHAT DO YOU THINK WE'VE BEEN DOING WITH THEM? YOU SAID YOURSELF THAT THEY SHOULD BE DEAD. SHOOTING THEM IN THE HEAD FIXES THAT.
WE'VE BEEN KILLING THEM.

KILLING THEM?! YOU'VE JUST BEEN KILLING THEM?!
WE'RE PUTTING THEM OUT OF THEIR MISERY, AND KEEPING THEM FROM KILLING US! THOSE THINGS AREN'T HUMAN. THEY'RE UNDEAD MONSTERS.
THEY'RE TRYING TO EAT US FOR GOD'S SAKE!
YOU DON'T KNOW WHY! YOU DON'T EVEN KNOW WHAT'S WRONG WITH THEM. NOBODY DOES. WE DON'T KNOW A DAMN THING ABOUT WHAT HAPPENED OR WHAT'S GOING ON.
I KNOW THOSE THINGS ARE TRYING TO KILL US--AND THAT THE LESS OF THEM THERE ARE OUT THERE THE SAFER WE'LL BE! AND I KNOW IT'S NOT SMART TO HAVE A MESS OF THEM PINNED UP NOT THIRTY FEET FROM YOUR GODDAMN HOUSE!

WE SHOULD GO IN THAT BARN RIGHT NOW AND SHOOT EVERY GODDAMN ONE OF THEM IN THE HEAD. IT'S NOT SAFE FOR THEM TO BE HERE! WE NEED TO KILL THEM BEFORE THEY KILL US!
MY SON IS IN THERE, GOD DAMMIT!
YOUR SON?
SHAWN WAS BITTEN. IT WAS BEFORE WE PUT UP THE BARRIER AROUND THE HOUSE. I--I COULDN'T HELP HIM, HE DIED AFTER A COUPLE DAYS... AND TURNED INTO ONE OF THEM.
I DIDN'T KNOW WHAT ELSE TO DO. SO I KEPT SHAWN IN THE BARN. HE TRIED TO ATTACK US... TO--KILL US. BUT I COULDN'T KILL HIM... I COULDN'T BRING MYSELF TO DO THAT. WHEN WE FOUND OTHERS... WE JUST... WE KEPT THEM TOO.
HERSHEL, I-- I'M REALLY SORRY. I TRULY AM. I CAN'T IMAGINE WHAT YOU'VE BEEN GOING THROUGH. IF I HAD LOST CARL-- I DON'T--I DON'T KNOW WHAT I WOULD HAVE DONE.

I DON'T THINK I COULD LIVE WITHOUT MY SON... BUT YOU'VE GOT TO LISTEN TO ME, HERSHEL. THAT THING IN THE BARN... IT'S NOT YOUR SON.
GET YOUR FUCKING HAND OFF ME!
THAP!
NOT MY SON?! WHAT MADE YOU SUCH A GODDAMN EXPERT?! I DON'T KNOW ABOUT YOU BUT THE ZOMBIES AROUND HERE DIDN'T COME WITH A FUCKING INSTRUCTION MANUAL!
WE DON'T KNOW A GODDAMN THING ABOUT THEM. WE DON'T KNOW WHAT THEY'RE THINKING--WHAT THEY'RE FEELING. WE DON'T KNOW IF IT'S A DISEASE OR SIDE EFFECTS OF SOME KIND OF CHEMICAL WARFARE! WE DON'T KNOW SHIT!
FOR ALL WE KNOW THESE THINGS COULD WAKE UP TOMORROW, HEAL UP, AND BE COMPLETELY NORMAL AGAIN!
WE JUST DON'T KNOW! YOU COULD HAVE BEEN MURDERING ALL THOSE PEOPLE YOU "PUT OUT OF THEIR MISERY."
THEY'RE DEAD. BEFORE THEY GET BACK UP--BEFORE THEY TRY TO EAT YOU--THEY DIE. YOU SAID YOU SAW YOUR SON DIE. HE'S DEAD. THOSE THINGS ARE ROTTING CORPSES WITH PIECES MISSING... THEY'RE NOT SICK PEOPLE... THEY'RE DEAD.
RICK, LISTEN. THESE THINGS COULD BE IN THE EARLY STAGES OF RECOVERY. THEY COULD BE HEALING... AND THAT'S WHY THINGS AREN'T WORKING RIGHT. THIS IS ALL COMPLETELY UNKNOWN TO US. WE'VE GOT NO CLUE HOW TO HANDLE THIS.
I DON'T WANT TO HAVE BLOOD ON MY HANDS IF WE FIND OUT THESE PEOPLE ARE ALIVE.

NO. THEY'RE DEAD! I'VE SEEN THOSE THINGS WITH THEIR DAMN GUTS HANGING OUT. WHAT YOU'RE SAYING DOESN'T MAKE A DAMN BIT OF SENSE.
RICK! WE'RE GUESTS HERE, MAN. WE AREN'T MAKING THE RULES.
JUST STOP THIS.
YOU'RE RIGHT, TYREESE. SORRY.
HOW MANY DO YOU HAVE IN THERE?
FOURTEEN. WE HAD TO RAID NEARBY HOUSES FOR SUPPLIES... BLANKETS, KEROSENE, AND WHAT NOT. ALL OUR NEIGHBORS HAD TURNED. IT'S MOSTLY THEM AND THEIR KIDS... AND A COUPLE WHO HAD WANDERED ONTO THE PROPERTY.
THEY CAN'T GET OUT OF THE BARN. WE'VE GOT THEM LOCKED UP TIGHT. WE'RE COMPLETELY SAFE HERE. YOU DON'T HAVE TO WORRY.
IF YOU SAY SO. I'M TRUSTING YOU ON THIS ONE.
I HOPE YOU'RE RIGHT.
...

ALLEN?

YOU DOING OKAY?

I DON'T KNOW, RICK. IT'S BEEN A *WHILE* SINCE I'VE HAD A FRAME OF REFERENCE FOR *"OKAY."*

HOW *LONG* YOU PLANNING ON STAYING OUT *HERE?* IT'S PRETTY *COLD.*

I JUST CAN'T SLEEP IN THERE, Y'KNOW. I SIT AND THINK ABOUT HOW WE BOTH USED TO SLEEP IN THAT AREA IN FRONT OF THE COUCH AND HOW *SHE'S* NOT *THERE* ANYMORE.

I CAN'T STOP THINKING ABOUT HER.

LAST NIGHT... I *SWEAR* I HEARD DONNA TALKING TO ME. I WAS LYING THERE TRYING TO SLEEP AND SHE JUST KEPT SAYING "TAKE CARE OF MY BOYS." IT WAS CLEAR AS DAY... IT WAS LIKE SHE WAS SITTING *RIGHT NEXT* TO ME.
I THINK I'M LOSING MY MIND.

YOU'LL GET THROUGH THIS, MAN. DON'T WORRY.

I DON'T KNOW MAN... SOMETIMES... I THINK ABOUT HOW MUCH I WANT TO DIE AND IT-- SCARES ME.
I LOVE MY BOYS... I KNOW THEY NEED ME BUT SOMETIMES I JUST THINK IT'D BE EASIER, Y'KNOW.
YOU'VE GOT TO PULL IT TOGETHER, ALLEN. YOU'VE GOT EVERY RIGHT TO BE SAD, MAKE NO MISTAKE ABOUT IT... BUT YOU'VE GOT TO BE THERE FOR YOUR SONS. THEY NEED YOU.
YOU DON'T--
OH, UH--HEY, GUYS. I COULDN'T SLEEP. I'M COMING OUT TO GET SOME... AIR.
CAREFUL, GLENN. IT'S PRETTY DARK OUT TONIGHT.
DON'T WORRY, RICK. I WON'T WANDER OFF TOO FAR.
I KNOW WHAT YOU'RE SAYING, RICK. IT'S JUST HARD. EVERYTHING'S SO DAMN HARD.
I KNOW, ALLEN... NOTHING'S EASY ANYMORE.
NOTHING.

MORNING, HERSHEL.
OH, HEY. GOOD MORNING, YOURSELF.
DID YOUR CREW SLEEP OKAY LAST NIGHT?
YEAH, THEY HAD A LITTLE EXTRA ROOM IN THE RV SINCE LORI AND I STAYED WITH CARL IN YOUR HOUSE LAST NIGHT.
THEY GOT AS MUCH SLEEP AS EVER, I MEAN. WE DON'T GET MUCH SLEEP ANY MORE, ANY OF US.
I CAN'T IMAGINE HOW YOU PEOPLE MADE IT OUT AT THAT CAMP OF YOURS. I FEEL INSECURE ENOUGH SLEEPING IN MY HOUSE.
I KNOW WHAT YOU MEAN. I HAVEN'T HAD A GOOD NIGHT'S SLEEP IN QUITE SOME TIME.
LISTEN, MAN... I WANTED TO APOLOGIZE FOR LAST NIGHT. I REALLY DIDN'T MEAN TO JUMP YOUR SHIT LIKE THAT. I'VE BEEN A LITTLE ON EDGE SINCE CARL GOT SHOT AND I WAS WAY OUT OF LINE.
I UNDERSTAND. WE'RE ALL A LITTLE ON EDGE, IT'S ONLY NATURAL, I DIDN'T TAKE OFFENSE.
STILL, I JUST WANTED TO LET YOU KNOW THAT I REALLY DO APPRECIATE ALL YOU'VE DONE FOR CARL, AND YOU ALLOWING US TO STAY HERE.

DON'T MENTION IT. I'M JUST DOING WHAT I CAN TO HELP MY FELLOW MAN.
WELL, ANYWAY... I WANTED TO GIVE YOU AND YOUR FAMILY SOME OF OUR GUNS. WE RAIDED A GUN STORE WHILE WE WERE IN ATLANTA AND WE GOT A LOT OF THEM.
WE'VE GOT SOME EXTRAS WE CAN SPARE. THREE PISTOLS AND A RIFLE AND WE FIGURED YOU COULD USE THEM. WE'VE GOT BULLETS TOO, BUT NOT TOO MANY.
WELL THANKS, RICK. I HOPE WE DON'T GET A LOT OF USE OUT OF THEM BUT I'M SURE THEY'LL COME IN HANDY IF WE NEED THEM.
I'M GOING TO BE DOING SOME TARGET SHOOTING WITH SOME OF OUR PEOPLE--THE KIDS MOSTLY AND YOU'RE WELCOME TO TAG ALONG. I'LL BE TEACHING BASIC GUN SAFETY AS WELL. THE LAST THING WE NEED ARE UNTRAINED PEOPLE CARRYING AROUND GUNS ON TOP OF ALL THE OTHER DANGERS OUT HERE.
SHOULD I EXPECT YOU?
LACEY, ARNOLD... AND I GUESS, MAGGIE WOULD PROBABLY BE UP FOR THAT. I DON'T WANT THE OTHERS INVOLVED. THEY'RE JUST TOO YOUNG TO BE CARRYING FIREARMS, YOUR SON CARL SEEMS TO BE FINE WITH HIS BUT MY KIDS DIDN'T GROW UP AROUND THEM LIKE I ASSUME HE DID.
I UNDERSTAND. I'LL ROUND UP EVERYONE THIS AFTERNOON.
YOU MIGHT WANT TO ASK PATRICA, OTIS' GIRL, IF SHE WANTS TO COME. I KNOW IT'D MAKE HER FEEL A LOT SAFER IF SHE DIDN'T HAVE TO RELY ON OTIS FOR PROTECTION.
RIGHT.

HEY, ALLEN.
CAN'T YOU TAKE A **HINT?** I HAVE **NOTHING** TO SAY TO YOU. YOU WANT TO RUN YOUR MOUTH AND GIVE PEOPLE ADVICE ON THINGS YOU **OBVIOUSLY** DON'T KNOW SHIT ABOUT... GO DO IT SOMEWHERE ELSE.
NOW HOLD ON JUST A DAMN--
NO, DALE. IT'S **OKAY.** LET IT GO.
I'M **SORRY,** ALLEN. I DIDN'T MEAN TO PISS YOU OFF.
YOU COULD HAVE **FOOLED** ME.

SOPHIA'S IN THERE TALKING WITH CARL AGAIN. I SWEAR... A FEW MORE YEARS AND WE'RE GOING TO HAVE TO KEEP AN EYE ON THOSE TWO. THEY'RE GETTING ALONG A LITTLE TOO WELL FOR THEIR AGE.
HEY, WHERE'D YOU GET THAT?
OH, THE BOOK? HERSHEL'S OLDEST DAUGHTER, LACEY HAS QUITE THE COLLECTION. I DIDN'T REALIZE HOW MUCH I MISSED READING. IT'S FUNNY HOW WE DON'T REALLY REALIZE THE THINGS WE'RE MISSING.
SPEAK FOR YOURSELF... I'D KILL FOR A VIKINGS GAME AND I'VE BEEN THINKING ABOUT THAT NONSTOP FOR WEEKS.
I HEAR YOU. I'D LOVE TO KNOW HOW THE RAIDERS ARE DOING. IF THERE'S ANY TEAM THAT COULD SURVIVE THIS... IT'S THEM.
HEY, LISTEN... CHRIS AND JULIE ARE GOING TO BE SHOOTING WITH US LATER TODAY, RIGHT? ARE THEY GOING TO BE CARRYING THEIR GUNS AT ALL TIMES?
I DON'T KNOW, MAN. I WANT THEM TO BE SAFE AND FEEL SAFE BUT I DON'T THINK THEY'RE READY TO HAVE GUNS ON THEM AT ALL TIMES. MAYBE AFTER A FEW PRACTICE SESSIONS ONCE I THINK THEY'VE GOT A GOOD HANDLE ON THINGS... BUT I'M NOT EVEN SURE I'LL BE COMFORTABLE WITH IT THEN.
THEY'RE TEENAGERS... I DON'T KNOW WHAT'S GOING THROUGH THEIR HEADS.
READING YOU LOUD AND CLEAR. SEE WHAT WE'VE GOT TO LOOK FORWARD TO, CAROL?
NOT ME. I'VE TALKED IT OVER WITH SOPHIA AND SHE'S SKIPPING RIGHT OVER TO HER EARLY TWENTIES.

YOU ABOUT READY? I'M GIVING YOU GUYS SOME LOW CALIBER GUNS SO THEY'LL BE A LITTLE EASIER TO HANDLE.
LET'S DO IT!
YEAH. THIS'LL BE FUN!
PKOW!
THIS ISN'T A GAME, JULIE. THIS IS SERIOUS STUFF. YOU LISTEN TO RICK AND DO EVERYTHING HE SAYS.
SHE KNOWS, MAN. YOU DON'T HAVE TO WORRY. WE'RE TAKING THIS SERIOUSLY.
GOOD TO KNOW. THANKS, CHRIS.
PTANG!
NICE ONE, MAN.
THANKS, BUT MY TEACHER DESERVES ALL THE CREDIT.

WHOA, WHOA! STOP SHOOTING!! STOP RIGHT NOW!
WHAT'S THE PROBLEM, HERSHEL?
THE THOMPSON'S HOUSE IS JUST ON THE OTHER SIDE OF THAT TREE LINE!
YOUR BULLETS ARE PROBABLY RIPPING RIGHT THROUGH THEIR HOUSE!
YOU CAN'T KEEP FIRING IN THAT DIRECTION!
JEEZ, SORRY ABOUT THAT. I HAD NO IDEA. THE THOMPSON'S HUH? THEY, UH...
ARE THEY IN YOUR BARN?
THAT'S NOT THE POINT! I DON'T WANT THEIR HOUSE TO BE DESTROYED. YOU CAN'T JUST--
THAT'S NOT WHAT I MEANT. I DIDN'T--
WHAT? WHAT'S GOING ON?

OH.
DAMN.
I THINK I CAN GET IT FROM HERE.
NO!
I CAN'T LET YOU SHOOT HIM. THERE'S ONLY ONE... HE'LL BE EASY TO GET INTO THE BARN.
JESUS.
BE CAREFUL, MAN. I DON'T NEED TO TELL YOU HOW DANGEROUS A BITE FROM ONE OF THESE SUCKERS IS.
HUMNGG!
I'VE DONE THIS A FEW TIMES BEFORE, YOU KNOW. THEY'RE ONLY REALLY DANGEROUS WHEN THERE'S MORE THAN ONE.

GO OVER THERE AND GET HIS ATTENTION.
OVER HERE, UGLY!
GOT YOU!
LOOKS LIKE YOU'VE GOT YOUR OWN LITTLE SYSTEM.
PIECE OF CAKE.
LACEY, ARNOLD... I'M GOING TO NEED YOUR HELP GETTING HIM IN THE BARN.
GUB.
GO AROUND BACK AND DISTRACT THE OTHERS WHILE I THROW THIS ONE IN.

TWACK!
OH SHIT!
HERSHEL!
DAD!
ACK. UGH.
I'M COMING DAD!!

RUNGH!
OH GOD! OH, PLEASE GOD!
NO!
WHUMP!
LORI! MAKE SURE ALL THE KIDS ARE IN THE HOUSE AND KEEP THEM THERE!
STAY INSIDE!
CHRIS! JULIE! INTO THE HOUSE WITH LORI!
NO!
NOT MY FATHER!
NOT MY FATHER!
HUNGH.
GRAR!
AAAGG!
ARNOLD!

SHAWN, NO! PLEASE SON! HE'S YOUR BROTHER! DON'T DO THIS!
YOU'VE GOT TO REMEMBER!
DADDY!
MAGGY STOP!!
BLAM!
LET GO OF ME!!
FWOP!
BLAM!
BLAM!
NO!
NO!
BLAM!
DADDY?!

AKK!
*

DADDY?
YOUR GUN.

DADDY?

BLAM!
I'M SORRY, SHAWN.

BLAM!

BLAM!
I'M SORRY, ARNOLD.

I'M SORRY.
BLAM!
I'M SORRY.
HERSHEL! NO!
...
I'M SO SORRY.

YOU WERE RIGHT.

DAD. MISTER GRIMES NEVER TOOK OUR GUNS BACK AFTER TARGET PRACTICE. I DON'T WANT YOU TO GET MAD AT US FOR STILL HAVING THEM LATER... SO WE'RE GIVING THEM TO YOU.
RICK'S HAD A LOT ON HIS HANDS TODAY, JULIE. I'LL JUST--
YOU KNOW WHAT? HOLD ONTO THEM. YOU'LL BE SAFER WITH THEM. I JUST DON'T WANT TO SEE THEM OUT UNLESS IT'S AN EMERGENCY, KEEP THEM HOLSTERED AT ALL TIMES.
OKAY.
FINALLY. I THOUGHT THAT BASTARD WOULD NEVER LET US HAVE GUNS.
IT'S GOING TO BE SO MUCH EASIER NOW.
YES. WE'LL DO IT AS SOON AS THE TIME IS RIGHT. I LOVE YOU, CHRIS.
I LOVE YOU, TOO.

MORNING, HON'.
YOU SLEEP OKAY? I GOTTA SAY... THIS BED IS REALLY DOING WONDERS FOR ME. EVEN WITH ALL THREE OF US SQUEEZING INTO IT, I'M SLEEPING BETTER THAN I HAVE IN--
YOU OKAY?
NO. MORNING SICKNESS... IT'S COMING AT ME FULL FORCE TODAY. I DON'T--
ULP!
MOM THROWING UP AGAIN?
YEP.
OH.

MAGGIE, I--
WHAT THE HELL ARE YOU DOING?!
OH, SIR! UH... I REALLY DIDN'T WANT--YOUR DAUGHTER AND I-- WE--
I'M SORRY!
NOT YET YOU AREN'T!

DADDY-- NO!
AND YOU! WHAT HAVE YOU DONE, MAGGIE? LACEY, ARNOLD, AND SHAWN HAVEN'T BEEN IN THE GROUND TWENTY-FOUR HOURS AND YOU'RE DOING THIS?
YOU MAKE ME SICK!
HEY!
GLENN AND I ARE IN LOVE, DADDY. I WANTED TO TELL YOU BEFORE BUT I JUST COULDN'T! WE LOVE EACH OTHER AND THERE'S NOTHING YOU CAN DO ABOUT THAT.
I'M NINETEEN! I'M OLD ENOUGH TO DO WHATEVER I WANT!
HE SLEPT HERE LAST NIGHT BECAUSE I ASKED HIM TO. I--I JUST... I'VE NEVER SLEPT ALONE IN THIS ROOM BEFORE!
I COULDN'T-- NOT WITH LACEY GONE. I NEEDED SOMEBODY TO BE HERE.
...

DALE? YOU COMING?
YEAH, IN A MINUTE. I JUST WANTED TO CLEAN UP A LITTLE. REMEMBER WHEN THIS WAS OUR PLACE--BEFORE EVERYONE ELSE STARTED SLEEPING IN HERE? THAT WAS NICE.
I DON'T THINK I'M EVER GOING TO GET THE SMELL OUT OF IT. I THINK IT'S SEEPED INTO THE WALLS. THIS PLACE IS A WRECK.
ERMA WOULD THROW A FIT IF SHE COULD SEE IT.
I'M SORRY. I KNOW YOU DON'T LIKE IT WHEN I MENTION HER.
NO. SHE WAS YOUR WIFE. I UNDERSTAND. IT'S JUST THAT IT REMINDS ME THAT SHE'S ALWAYS ON YOUR MIND, AND I--
DON'T THINK OF IT THAT WAY, ANDREA. I WAS MARRIED TO ERMA FOR ALMOST FORTY YEARS. YOU CAN'T BE JEALOUS OF MY MEMORIES.
I KNOW, DALE... I KNOW.
I LOVE YOU, ANDREA. I REALLY LOVE YOU.
I SWEAR.

I DON'T THINK THIS IS A ONE DAY JOB. NOT BY A LONG SHOT. I'M SORRY, MAN--BUT I THINK YOU'VE GOT A FEW MORE NIGHTS IN THE RV.
LOOKS THAT WAY TO ME TOO. ALTHOUGH, KNOWING THAT I'LL BE OUT OF THAT PLACE SOON WILL KEEP ME GOING. IT'LL BE GOOD TO KNOW I'VE GOT A PILE OF HAY WAITING TO REPLACE MY SPOT ON THE FLOOR IN FRONT OF THE COUCH.
HANG IN THERE, BUDDY. WE'LL HAVE THIS BARN CLEAN IN A FEW YEARS...
HEY ALLEN, HOW YOU DOING?
YOU OKAY?
NO, RICK--AND I PROBABLY NEVER WILL BE, BUT THAT'S OKAY. I'M KEEPING IT TOGETHER, FOR DONNA, FOR THE KIDS. THAT'S WHAT SHE WOULD HAVE WANTED.
Y'KNOW--DONNA WAS EIGHT YEARS OLDER THAN ME. SHE WAS ALWAYS WISER--MORE LEVEL-HEADED... SHE ALWAYS KNEW WHAT TO DO, OR WAS ABLE TO CONVINCE ME THAT SHE DID. I DON'T KNOW HOW I'M GOING TO SEE THOSE BOYS TO ADULTHOOD WITHOUT HER. I REALLY DON'T KNOW WHAT I'M GOING TO DO. BUT I'M GOING TO TRY.
I'M GOING TO DO MY BEST.
FOR HER.

SORRY YOU ASKED?
NO-- YEAH--IT'S NOT LIKE THAT. I JUST DON'T KNOW WHAT TO SAY TO YOU NOW.
ASIDE FROM A FEW MINOR THINGS--THE STRESS FROM THE PREGNANCY... I'M DOING GOOD. I'M WITH MY WIFE AND SON... WE'RE SAFE... I DON'T HAVE MUCH TO COMPLAIN ABOUT.
I CAN'T PRETEND LIKE I KNOW WHAT YOU'RE GOING THROUGH... I CAN'T SAY, "YEAH, I KNOW HOW YOU FEEL." BECAUSE I DON'T. I JUST DON'T KNOW WHAT TO SAY.
YOU DON'T HAVE TO SAY ANYTHING, RICK.
YOU'RE NOT GOING TO FIX IT. YOU'RE NOT GOING TO MAKE ME FEEL BETTER. I KNOW YOU CARE. THAT'S SOMETHING. THAT'S ENOUGH.
OKAY. UNDERSTOOD.
I--
DAMMIT! THIS IS STUPID!
WE'RE CLEANING THIS PLACE UP SO WE CAN LIVE IN IT?! WE'RE GOING TO LIVE IN A BARN FOR THE REST OF OUR LIVES?!
HERSHEL IS A REASONABLE GUY. I KNOW HE JUST LOST TWO OF HIS KIDS... BUT IF THERE'S EXTRA ROOM IN THAT PLACE I DON'T SEE WHY WE CAN'T STAY THERE.
HE'S LETTING LORI AND I SHARE THAT ROOM WITH CARL... YOU AND THE TWINS COULD SLEEP IN THERE WITH US... IF THERE WAS JUST ONE MORE ROOM, SPLITTING TWO ROOMS BETWEEN US WOULD BE BETTER THAN SLEEPING IN A BARN.
I'M GOING TO FIND HERSHEL.

HERSHEL?
YOU GOT A MINUTE?
LONG AS WHAT YOU'RE ABOUT TO SAY CAN BE SAID IN FRONT OF A HORSE, I'M ALL EARS.
HERSHEL. I KNOW IT'S NOT THE BEST TIME TO BE BRINGING THIS UP-- WITH WHAT HAPPENED YESTERDAY AND ALL, BUT I WAS THINKING...
ALLEN AND I ARE BACK THERE CLEANING OUT THE BARN SO WE CAN SLEEP IN IT AND I JUST DON'T SEE THE POINT OF IT ALL. WE AIN'T SLEEPING IN THE BARN FOREVER AND IF THERE'S EXTRA ROOM IN YOUR HOUSE NOW I DON'T SEE WHY WE CAN'T--
NO. ABSOLUTELY NOT. YOU'RE WELCOME HERE WHILE YOUR BOY HEALS. WHEN HE'S DONE, YOU GO. YOU'RE NOT MOVING IN HERE. YOU'RE NOT TAKING MY SONS' ROOM.
NO.
WHAT?
NO.
NOW LEAVE ME ALONE.

EASY NOW!
I'VE HAD PLENTY OF CRACKED RIBS IN MY DAY--THEY BREAK REAL EASY.
HUH?
BIG, TOUGH MAN LIKE YOU AND I'M LEANING BACK TOO HARD?
WHAT CAN I SAY--MY RUGGEDNESS IS TOTAL BULLSHIT.
OKAY, TRY NOW. LEAN BACK.
BETTER?
YEAH.
I'M SO GLAD I FOUND YOU, CAROL. EVERYTHING IS PERFECT.
YEAH, IT--QUICK... KNOCK ON WOOD OR SOMETHING.
OH, COME ON.
I'M SERIOUS. YOU NEVER KNOW WHAT'S GOING TO HAPPEN NEXT.

LORI-- DON'T!
HEY!
YOU'RE THROWING US OUT?! WHY?! WHAT THE HELL DID WE DO, DAMMIT?!
HOW CAN YOU LET US STAY HERE FOR WEEKS AND THEN JUST TURN US AWAY?
I NEVER INVITED YOU TO LIVE HERE. I'M LETTING YOU STAY HERE WHILE YOUR SON HEALS. I DON'T HAVE ENOUGH FOOD TO FEED ALL OF US LONG-TERM. I HAVE TO LOOK OUT FOR MY FAMILY.
YOU MEAN BY KEEPING A DAMN BARN FULL OF ZOMBIES NEXT DOOR?! OR DO YOU MEAN YOU'RE GOING TO START LOOKING OUT FOR YOUR FAMILY FROM NOW ON?
IF WE HADN'T BEEN HERE--AND GIVEN YOU OUR EXTRA GUNS--YOU'D ALL BE DEAD RIGHT NOW! BUT YOU'RE GOING TO KICK US OUT?
WHAT DO YOU WANT FROM ME? I SAVED YOUR BOY'S LIFE AND I LOST TWO OF MY OWN. HAVEN'T I GIVEN YOU ENOUGH?!
WE DIDN'T KILL YOUR KIDS--IF ANYONE HERE IS RESPONSIBLE FOR THAT IT'S YOU AND YOUR STUPIDITY!
YOU'VE RUN YOUR MOUTH ENOUGH, WOMAN!
DAD, NO!

THAT'S ENOUGH!
DON'T YOU FUCKING TOUCH ME!
YOU WERE GOING TO HIT ME?! WHAT THE FUCK IS WRONG WITH YOU?!
I LOST THREE KIDS YESTERDAY, YOU STUPID BITCH! THREE! TODAY I FIND ONE OF YOU FUCKING MY DAUGHTER--THEN YOUR HUSBAND IS ASKING TO TAKE MY KIDS' ROOMS! AND NOW YOU'RE ON MY ASS BECAUSE I WON'T LET YOU FREE-LOADERS EAT ALL MY DAMN FOOD AND FILL UP MY HOUSE!
WHERE THE HELL DO YOU GET OFF?! THIS IS MY FUCKING HOUSE. I HAVE A FAMILY TO LOOK AFTER. I DON'T OWE YOU SHIT!
I DON'T OWE YOU SHIT.
WE NEVER SAID YOU DID, HERSHEL.

WE THOUGHT YOU WERE LETTING US STAY HERE. YOU NEVER MENTIONED THIS BEING TEMPORARY, GODDAMN IT.
DO YOU HAVE ANY IDEA WHAT IT'S LIKE OUT THERE? HUNTING FOR FOOD? CRAMMING INTO THAT FUCKING RV? GETTING ATTACKED BY THOSE MONSTERS AT EVERY GODDAMN TURN?
NOT.
MY.
PROBLEM.
I'VE GOT TO LOOK OUT FOR MY KIDS.
WHAT ABOUT OUR KIDS?
YOU'VE GOT A FENCE--A HOUSE--YOU'RE SAFE HERE. WE COULD HELP YOU GROW MORE FOOD IN THE SUMMER, WE COULD MAKE IT WORK!
WE COULD HAVE A LIFE HERE. YOU CAN'T JUST SEND US BACK OUT THERE. WE COULD DIE! YOU'RE SENTENCING US TO DEATH!
YOU CAN'T DO THIS!
LORI, PLEASE.
IT'S GOING TO BE OKAY.

I WANT YOU OUT OF HERE.
RIGHT NOW.
HERSHEL-- WHAT THE FUCK?!
I WANT THEM TO LEAVE, OTIS. EVERYTHING WENT TO HELL AFTER THEY CAME.
WE WERE DOING FINE BEFORE THEY GOT HERE.
THEY FUCKED EVERYTHING UP.
FINE. WE'LL LEAVE.
WE'RE LEAVING.

HERSHEL? YOU IN THERE? I WANNA TALK TO YOU.
I AIN'T GOT NO CLUE WHAT'S RUNNING AROUND IN YOUR HEAD, MAN--BUT YOU COULDA SHOT THAT MAN.
YOU HEAR ME IN THERE?
MAN, I UNDERSTAND YOU WANTING THEM TO GO--BUT THAT AIN'T NO WAY TO BE TREATIN' ANYBODY. YOU GOTTA APOLOGIZE TO RICK BEFORE HE GOES, MAN.
YOU GOTTA--
YOU IN THERE?
HERSHEL?
HERSHEL!
I WAS GOING TO SHOOT THAT MAN, OTIS. I WAS GOING TO PULL THAT TRIGGER IF HE RESISTED IN ANY WAY. I WANTED THEM TO LEAVE THAT BAD.
I ALMOST PULLED THE TRIGGER. I ALMOST KILLED A MAN.
I THINK I'VE LOST MY MIND.

DID YOU SAY GOODBYE TO THAT GIRL?
NO.
NO? WHAT DO YOU MEAN?
I'M NOT GOING. I'M IN LOVE, RICK--OR AS CLOSE AS I'M LIABLE TO GET. I DON'T KNOW IF I'LL EVER FIND ANOTHER WOMAN LIKE MAGGIE. SHE TALKED IT OVER WITH HER FATHER... HE SAID IT'S OKAY.
I'M NOT LEAVING.
OH, GLENN... I... UH.
I THINK PART OF THE REASON I DIDN'T HAVE ANY PROBLEMS RUNNING INTO ATLANTA FOR SUPPLIES WAS BECAUSE I DIDN'T REALLY CARE IF I LIVED OR DIED. I WAS SCARED...BUT I DIDN'T CARE THAT I WAS SCARED. I THINK I ALMOST WANTED TO DIE--JUST TO GET IT OVER WITH.
I DON'T FEEL THAT WAY NOW. NOT WITH MAGGIE.
I GOTTA STAY, RICK. I DON'T WANT TO FEEL LIKE THAT ANYMORE. I DON'T WANT TO BE ALONE.
NO. GLENN... I COMPLETELY UNDERSTAND. I WANT YOU TO BE HAPPY.
I AM HAPPY. I DIDN'T THINK IT WAS POSSIBLE, BUT I AM.
YOU WANT TO COME IN, SAY GOODBYE TO EVERYONE?
NO. JUST GO. I'M TERRIBLE WITH GOOD-BYES.

SIGH
HERE WE GO AGAIN.
SHUT UP.
I'D KILL FOR SOME PICKLES.
I'D KILL FOR ANYTHING. WE NEED TO FIND SOME FOOD. QUICK.
THIS HUNTING AND FORAGING STUFF JUST ISN'T CUTTING IT--NOT BY A LONGSHOT.

CAN I HAVE SOME MORE, MOMMY?

I'M SORRY, SOPHIA. THAT'S ALL WE'VE GOT. WE DON'T HAVE ANY LEFT.

BUT I'M STILL HUNGRY.

ENERAL STORE
NOTHING?
NOTHING WE CAN *EAT*.
DINER

WE'RE OUT OF GAS. WE HAVEN'T SEEN ANY STRANDED CARS FOR A WHILE. I WANT EVERYONE TO SPREAD OUT, LOOK FOR CARS, ANYWHERE. IF YOU SEE ANY NEARBY HOUSES, LET US KNOW, THERE'S GOT TO BE SOMETHING AROUND HERE WE COULD AT LEAST SPEND A FEW NIGHTS IN TO GET OUT OF THE RV.
KEEP YOUR GUNS HANDY. IF YOU SEE ANY ZOMBIES, DON'T LET YOURSELF GET SURROUNDED. DON'T FORGET, WE'RE SMARTER AND FASTER. DON'T LOSE YOUR COOL. RUN IF YOU HAVE TO.
IF YOU FIND ANY FOOD... BRING IT BACK SO WE CAN SHARE IT. REMEMBER THE KIDS.
IF YOU FIND ANYTHING, FOOD, GAS, WATER, OR SHELTER, COME BACK TO THE RV AND HONK THE HORN. ALLEN WILL BE HERE WITH THE KIDS.
IF YOU DON'T FIND ANYTHING, BE BACK HERE BEFORE DARK.
WE'VE ONLY GOT A FEW HOURS.
FINALLY, ALONE TIME.
DON'T GET ANY IDEAS. I'M STARVING. WE'RE NOT DOING ANYTHING UNTIL WE FIND SOME FOOD.
IF I COULD GET AWAY WITH IT... I'D GNAW A PIECE OFF OF YOU.
FUNNY GIRL.
YOU KIDS THESE DAYS--I JUST DON'T GET YOUR HUMOR.
UH-HUH.
ANOTHER DAY WITHOUT FOOD AND NONE OF US WILL BE LAUGHING.

=UNG=
ARE YOU O--?
WE'VE GOT TO SHOW RICK AND THE REST.
YEAH. OH, WOW.
HONK! HONK! HONK! HONK!
OW.
THAT WAS QUICK. WHAT DID YOU FIND?
YOU'LL SEE, JUST FOLLOW ME.
OH, MAN.

OH, NO--IT'S FULL OF THEM. WE CAN'T GO IN THERE.
IT MAY NOT BE SAFE NOW BUT LOOK AT THAT FENCE. IT COULD BE MADE TO BE SAFE. THAT PLACE HAS BEDS, SUPPLIES, CLOTHES, MAYBE EVEN SOME FOOD--IT HAS TO.
LOOK AT ALL THE LAND INSIDE THE FENCE... SAFE, SECURE. WE COULD MAKE A LIFE HERE.
NO... WE CAN CLEAN IT UP. THERE CAN'T BE THAT MANY INSIDE. THIS IS TOO GOOD A PLACE TO PASS UP. WE CAN MAKE THIS WORK.

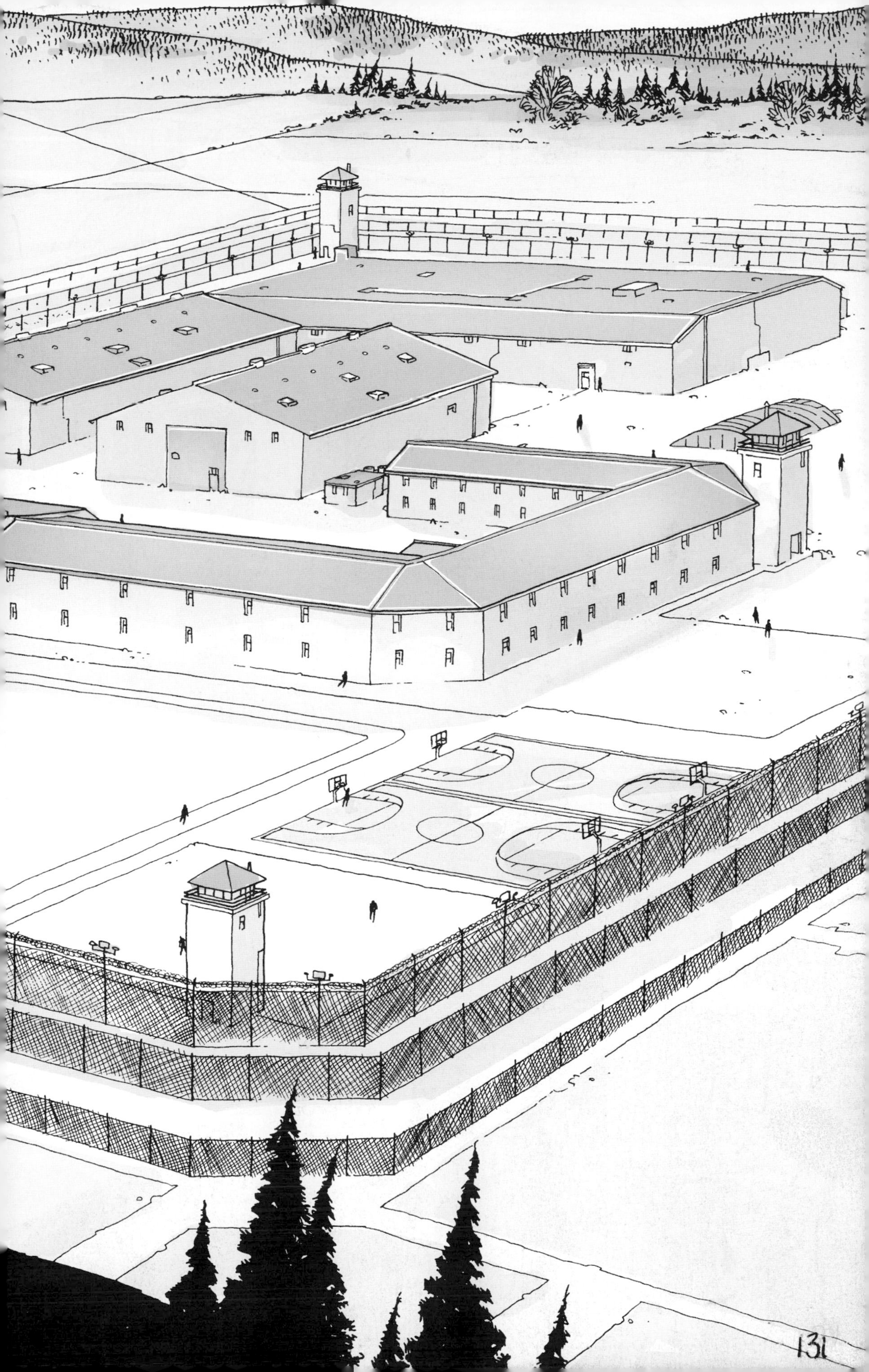

IT'S PERFECT.
WE'RE HOME.

AFTERWORD BY SIMON PEGG

While other monsters clamour for attention with capes and claws and bandages, the zombie has embedded itself into our consciousnesses with little more that a stumble and a moan. Metaphorically, this classic creature embodies a number of our greatest fears. Most obviously, it is our own death, personified. The physical manifestation of that thing we fear the most. More subtly, the zombie represents a number of our deeper insecurities. The fear that deep down, we may be little more than animals, concerned only with appetite. Zombies can represent the threat of collectivism against individuality. The notion that we might be swallowed up and forgotten, our special-ness devoured by the crowd.

Oddly, those rotten bastards also give us hope. The undead maybe tenacious, single minded and as relentless as lava, but they are also stupid and slow; ineffectual and inept. You don't have to be Van Helsing, or even Peter Venkman to throw down with a zombie. Anyone with a pulse can step up. As long as you keep your head, defeating a zombie is not an insurmountable task. You don't need spells, or stakes, or silver bullets, you just need your wits and a weapon. A gun is good, but most blunt objects will do, things we might have around the house or the garden. It is perhaps this combination of hope in the face of terror, that makes the zombie so attractive to us. The idea that we could ourselves, beat death. Beat it until its brains come out of its ears.

With The Walking Dead, Robert Kirkman has brilliantly captured the spirit of George A. Romero's definitive vision of the modern zombie and applied it to his own epic tale of survival. I would imagine everybody reading this has at some time or another asked themselves the question: What would I do? How would I survive if it was me against them? Whilst our favourite zombie movies always seem to finish far too quickly, leaving us wondering what happened next, Kirkman is able to savour the journey and explore the many dangers and dilemmas facing his increasingly diminishing and outnumbered band of survivors. Often, as in some of the best zombie stories, the ghouls themselves are merely bit part players, a context in which to play out the human story. Our real concerns are for the people that remain, for their future and by proxy, our own.

The Walking Dead brilliantly captures the simple truth that in the face of Armageddon, the little things remain unchanged. We still love and hate the same people. We still like the same bands, get the horn, remain frightened of heights and spiders. Kirkman cleverly focuses his narrative on the enduring minutiae of human existence and uses a full blown zombie apocalypse to bring it into sharp relief. Often the roots of great fantasy are firmly embedded in the truth. It is this simple reality that makes The Walking Dead such an engrossing read.

Now, that may be just be a load of bullshit, film school speculation, but as we all know, it's unwise to underestimate a zombie. So if you're a fan who's just torn through this volume, devouring it hungrily, clawing at each page turn, desperate for the next morsel of information, go back to the beginning, take a big deep breath and start again. Savour it, think about it, re-evaluate it and like the best zombies, take it slow.

Simon Pegg
2004

FOR MORE OF THE WALKING DEAD

TRADEPAPERBACKS

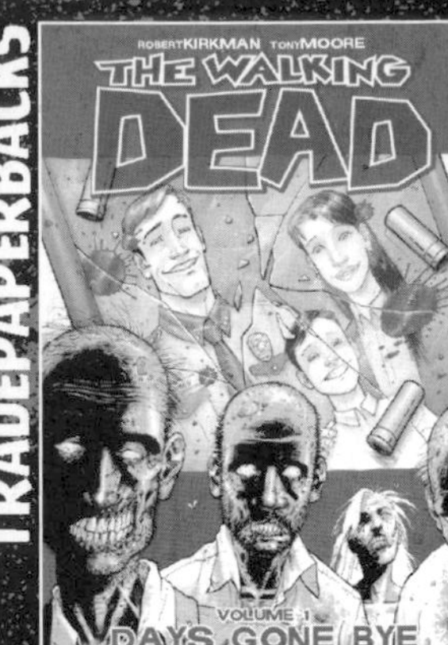

VOL. 1: DAYS GONE BYE TP
ISBN: 978-1-58240-672-5
$14.99
VOL. 2: MILES BEHIND US TP
ISBN: 978-1-58240-775-3
$14.99
VOL. 3: SAFETY BEHIND BARS TP
ISBN: 978-1-58240-805-7
$14.99
VOL. 4: THE HEART'S DESIRE TP
ISBN: 978-1-58240-530-8
$14.99
VOL. 5: THE BEST DEFENSE TP
ISBN: 978-1-58240-612-1
$14.99
VOL. 6: THIS SORROWFUL LIFE TP
ISBN: 978-1-58240-684-8
$14.99

VOL. 7: THE CALM BEFORE TP
ISBN: 978-1-58240-828-6
$14.99
VOL. 8: MADE TO SUFFER TP
ISBN: 978-1-58240-883-5
$14.99
VOL. 9: HERE WE REMAIN TP
ISBN: 978-1-60706-022-2
$14.99
VOL. 10: WHAT WE BECOME TP
ISBN: 978-1-60706-075-8
$14.99
VOL. 11: FEAR THE HUNTERS TP
ISBN: 978-1-60706-181-6
$14.99
VOL. 12: LIFE AMONG THEM TP
ISBN: 978-1-60706-254-7
$14.99

VOL. 13: TOO FAR GONE TP
ISBN: 978-1-60706-329-2
$14.99
VOL. 14: NO WAY OUT TP
ISBN: 978-1-60706-392-6
$14.99
VOL. 15: WE FIND OURSELVES TP
ISBN: 978-1-60706-440-4
$14.99
VOL. 16: A LARGER WORLD TP
ISBN: 978-1-60706-559-3
$14.99
VOL. 17: SOMETHING TO FEAR TP
ISBN: 978-1-60706-615-6
$14.99

HARDCOVERS

BOOK ONE HC
ISBN: 978-1-58240-619-0
$34.99
BOOK TWO HC
ISBN: 978-1-58240-698-5
$34.99
BOOK THREE HC
ISBN: 978-1-58240-825-5
$34.99
BOOK FOUR HC
ISBN: 978-1-60706-000-0
$34.99
BOOK FIVE HC
ISBN: 978-1-60706-171-7
$34.99
BOOK SIX HC
ISBN: 978-1-60706-327-8
$34.99
BOOK SEVEN HC
ISBN: 978-1-60706-439-8
$34.99
BOOK EIGHT HC
ISBN: 978-1-60706-593-7
$34.99

COMPENDIUMS

COMPENDIUM TP, VOL. 1
ISBN: 978-1-60706-076-5
$59.99
COMPENDIUM TP, VOL. 2
ISBN: 978-1-60706-596-8
$59.99

SPECIALTY BOOKS

THE WALKING DEAD: THE COVERS, VOL. 1 HC
ISBN: 978-1-60706-002-4
$24.99
THE WALKING DEAD SURVIVORS' GUIDE
ISBN: 978-1-60706-458-9
$12.99

OMNIBUS

OMNIBUS, VOL. 1
ISBN: 978-1-60706-503-6
$100.00
OMNIBUS, VOL. 2
ISBN: 978-1-60706-515-9
$100.00
OMNIBUS, VOL. 3
ISBN: 978-1-60706-330-8
$100.00
OMNIBUS, VOL. 4
ISBN: 978-1-60706-616-3
$100.00